The outer door flung open and in tripped a little blonde carrying as many bags as she probably weighed. He watched her struggle to close the door for a moment and was about to get up and help when half of what she was trying to hold slipped from her hands, scattering across the carpet.

Sighing loudly, she closed the door, now almost empty-handed. Turning around she looked at the notebooks and supplies all over the floor. She smirked at the man sitting in the waiting area. "That was rather graceful, wasn't it? Fall in the door and toss everything on the floor." Setting the rest of the bags on a chair, she knelt to start shoving things back into a bag.

Brent sat there for a moment. This was the woman that Jac didn't want the doc alone with? Snapping out of it, he got up and went over. Squatting down he began to pick up pencils and booklets that were scattered all over. She glanced up at him, the long wavy blonde hair half hiding her face, and smiled at him. The palest blue eyes he'd ever seen paralyzed his speech.

"Thank you." She flipped the hair out of her face and looked around to see if she'd missed anything. "I usually don't make such a dramatic entrance, really." She got back to her feet, setting the bags with the other ones on the chair.

Brent stood up and looked down at the tiny woman. Her appearance reminded him of a porcelain figurine. "No problem." He finally made his mouth say.

ANIMAL SENSES
1 *Heart*
2 *Scent*
3 *Passion*
4 *Courage*
5 *Solace*
6 *Faith*
7 *Spirit*
Coming soon:

8 Fury
9 Pride
10 Torment

MAGIC SEASONS ROMANCE
1 *Beltane Magic*
2 *Solstice Heat*
3 *Harvest Dreams*
4 *Autumn Dance*
5 *Winter Mist*

Dreams
Three steamy stories that started with a dream

Curses
Two tales of curses.

After the Silence

SINGLE TITLES
Solitary Witchling
Salvation
Café Serenity

Coming soon:

Outcasts

<u>**Writing As: J. Risk**</u>

REALMS BOOKS:

THE ALTEREALM SERIES
1 *The Huntress*
2 *The Seer*
3 *The Empath*
4 *The Witch*
5 *The Chronos*
6 *The Warrior*
7 *The Telepath*
8 *The Healer*
9 *The Kinetic*

THE SOLRELM SERIES
Coming soon:

Concealed

GEMINI LEAGUE
Coming soon

Dark Moon

DREAM VISIONS

Book II

Mystic Gifts Trilogy

BY

Jacqueline Paige

Published by Exordium Books (FRP)
Copyright © 2022 Roxane Kerr

Excerpts from *The Witch Within; Heart* by Jacqueline Paige, *The Huntress* by J. Risk copyright ©2015,2022 Roxane Kerr

ISBN: 978-1-990763-27-4

Prologue

She found herself standing in the kitchen and not sure why she was there. Blinking a few times, she focused on the room. No one else was in it. Turning quickly, she headed towards the stairs, almost running into her mother.

"I thought you were coming to get a snack?"

Felicity stared blankly at the floor. "I – uh – I forgot about a project." She turned and backed slowly towards the door. "I'll be back down after I get my outline finished." She turned and ran with rubber legs towards the stairs.

Closing her bedroom door, she leaned against it shaking. That was close. If they knew she was still having these – what? Dreams? Whatever, they would have her back in therapy faster than she could blink.

Taking a deep breath, she quickly walked into her enormous closet and closed the door behind her. She knelt on the floor and pulled the shoebox out from its hiding place under the bottom shelf. Pulling the notebook out, she flipped to the first blank page.

Closing her eyes, she wrote without really looking at it, what she could remember. It hadn't been anything terrible or earth-shattering, but she still wrote it down.

After she finished, she closed the notebook, then carefully hid it back in its secret place. Sitting back against the wall she wrapped her arms around her waist and hugged herself.

Still feeling a little shaky, she took a few deep breaths—at least she didn't pass out or throw up. They were happening more often, these vision things. She frowned; it was getting harder to hide the fact that she was still having them. So far, she'd been able to find a story fast enough to cover up anytime it had happened—headaches, upset stomach, or some forgotten project. So far, they were buying her excuses and mishaps, but she knew it was only a matter of time before she had a really strong one, and then she wouldn't be able to fake through what happened afterward.

She picked at the dress hanging on the back of the door; she wasn't going to think about how her parents treated her. Maybe she was some sort of weirdo, but weren't your parents supposed to love you no matter what?

One more year and she could leave and fade out of their overpriced world.

1

Sitting on the tiny bed, hugging his knees as tightly as he could against his chest, his eyes darted around the room. It was so dark and so quiet here--he just wanted to go home and see his mom. Someone would come; someone always did in the movies...

A creaking noise made him gasp; he quickly looked toward the door. Pushing himself back further into the musty corner, he watched and listened.

When it creaked again, he grabbed the thin blanket and dropped to lie down on the bed, squeezing his still damp eyes closed tightly.

Felicity blinked a few times and looked down. She was standing at her kitchen counter, hands grasping the edge so hard her knuckles were white. Sighing, pushing the straying blonde hair away from her face; her hand vibrating.

Closing her eyes, she took a calming breath. "I wished you would show me where sweetheart." Whispering out loud made her feel better, even knowing he would never hear her.

Rinsing her hands under the cool water, she patted some against her sweaty brow. Drying them quickly, she looked around for a moment trying to recall what she had been doing before the vision blocked out the rest of the world.

The kettle began to whistle, startling her. Unplugging it, she shook her head. *It could have been worse, you might have been cutting vegetables or something else that could result in coming out of it injured.*

If there was one thing she was thankful for it was that when it happened her body froze-- and that usually prevented her from too many serious injuries. Of course, it made life more complicated when it came to things like being in public or driving, both of which she tried to avoid.

Taking the cup of tea, she went over to the desk and pulled the tattered notebook from the drawer. Wanting to record every detail before she forgot any of it, she began jotting it down. Taking her time, she wrote carefully, making sure she described every little thing—even going as far as the crunching sound the old rusty cot frame made as the little boy moved.

Closing the book, she glanced at the stack of sketches briefly before she returned the book to the drawer and closed it.

Sipping her tea, she tried not to fall into the depression that sometimes followed the visions. The helpless feeling of seeing, and not being able to do anything. It had been a few months since she'd had any—they'd started again about a week ago. In the first few there had been two children, but she didn't know what happened to the sweet cherub-faced little girl that the boy had been so brave for.

Getting up, she walked over and looked out the window at the quiet evening outside. She wanted to know enough to alert the police before she moved on. Felicity had accepted that moving on was inevitable—again. The judge had been the most understanding so far and she would humor him by showing up for at least one of her ordered therapy sessions.

Looking away from the window, she rolled her eyes. Having been through it before, she knew how that would end, too. The therapist—of whichever qualifications this one had— would have all sorts of suggestions, theories, and of course, drugs.

Having been through it all before, she wasn't sure if she could do it again. Her parents actually once had wanted to help her, although Felicity knew it was more to save their social status than because of their love for her.

After five years of doctors, five years of treatments, and medications, she fled as soon as she was old enough to legally moved around the country on her own.

Winking at her reflection in the glass, she grinned. *Now many, many years later you're older and still fleeing.* Laughing to herself, she thought that in appearance she might not look your age, but inside she was ancient.

Setting the cup down on her worktable, she pulled the long wavy hair over her shoulder, quickly braiding it to stay out of her way. *Better get this story finished before we're on the road again.* Looking down at the animal cartoon sketches, she grinned. "Let's see what adventures we can get you into this time."

If someone had told her when she was younger, that she'd make a living by writing children's stories—she would have fallen over laughing. But, desperate to support herself without having to be in the public, this had been the only way. Of course, her publishers no longer asked questions; they were just happy that the series of books from the mysterious B. Woods was a huge success.

It was funny how money persuaded people to do things. The publisher was more than happy to wire her royalty payments to an account. She had never met them and kept all communications limited to emails.

Pausing, she stared at the keyboard for a moment. Shaking her head, she continued with the silly tale—promising to check the missing children's bulletin site again after she'd gotten some work done.

Her cell phone rang and made her jump in the chair; she rarely got phone calls— who would be calling her? Glancing at it, the art supply store name came up. Setting the phone back down, she let them leave a message. At least she'd have lots of supplies when she made her move this time. Looking out the window again, she wondered which direction she should choose this time. Sighing, she grimaced. *You're almost out of directions.*

~

With the text printing out, she went through the drawings to match them. *Just have to get these finished up and get them shipped.* Yawning, she glanced at the clock. She hadn't realized how late she had worked. Debating for a minute on whether she would make a late dinner or just go to bed, she rolled her eyes and headed back into the tiny kitchen. *You know you have to eat regularly Miss Dante, or the visions leave you weak as a mouse.*

As she made a small solitary meal, again, she couldn't fight the feelings of being alone. She was always alone, but from time to time it bothered her. For years she had hoped to find someone— just one person that would understand and believe her, fill the empty places in her life. Getting a glass of milk from the fridge, she set it beside the single plate on the small table. She'd given up that dream a long time ago. She'd moved past the age of twenty alone – so when thirty had followed the same way, she hadn't felt the melancholy of the isolation. Frowning, she refused to think of any number near forty. Thirty-five was as old as she was getting.

She didn't really taste a single bite of the food she chewed while thinking. A lot of her world was like that though—do what you need to get through it. Glancing over, she picked up the forms the judge had given her. Her own fault really, when the police had completely doubted her -- and looked at her like she'd just escaped the nearest mental facility. Instead of walking out without argument, she'd demanded to talk to someone higher up. How was she supposed to know a judge just happened to be there at the time? Since when did judges hang around at police stations?

They hadn't listened or given up any time to try to help the little girl and in turn for her trouble, she got to go see a professional to help her through her episodes. Anonymous – she knew she had to report things in an anonymous fashion – hadn't she learned that the hard way repeatedly? But the little girl in her vision had been so frightened, it had broken Felicity's heart and she couldn't stand it a moment longer.

Tossing the paperwork back onto the table, she got up to rinse her dishes. She'd go to the therapist– mostly to buy herself time so she wasn't arrested on some insubordinate charge. As soon as she had everything organized and packed, she'd move on.

Standing at the counter, she closed her eyes and prayed silently for a moment—that she wouldn't see the little girl or the little boy on the news anytime soon in some heart-wrenching morbid discovery. She couldn't deal with another one of those. Couldn't face sitting all alone crying, hearing how someone she had tried to help hadn't gotten it and she'd been left alone to regret once more that society didn't accept anything out of the ordinary.

2

Brent took his time going to work for a change. He'd spent yesterday with Reid, gathering up the little pieces to the dating site murders. With the evidence recovered from the homes of Howard and Lawson, the case was now air-tight and neither of them would be able to squirm their way out of a very long jail sentence.

Hopefully, the Captain would give them a few days off to rest, he smirked knowing he was just dreaming and a few days off weren't going to happen. Blowing out a breath, he pulled into the parking lot, noting the swarm of reporters was finally gone. A few easy cases would be a nice change. He smirked, knowing both Reid and him would get bored silly if it were easy, but it was still nice to think that might happen.

He heard the voices before he reached the office. As he stepped in the door, he saw Jacinda waving papers at Reid while Sandy leaned against the desk reading. Well, that was a change from coming down to the scowling, silent partner he was used to starting his days with.

"What do you mean there's something? Define something?" Reid crossed his arms over his chest and looked down at her.

Tossing the papers back on the table she put her hands on her hips, glaring up at him. "If I could define something – then most likely I wouldn't refer to it as *something*."

Brent smirked. She did have a point, not that his partner would admit it. Walking over, he stopped beside the Doctor, he leaned closer to her. "Have I missed something interesting?"

Sandy glanced away from the pages she was flipping through. "Yes, and I think it's my fault."

Jac turned around and looked at her. "It's not your fault. You were concerned and I said I'd check into it for you…"

"All night?" Reid went and sat behind his desk. Glancing at Brent he scowled. "The name you ran yesterday—she spent all night digging around."

Brent frowned. "Really? Other than a few minor incidents, no convictions – I didn't think there was too much to find out."

Sandy handed him the papers she'd been reading. "You'd be wrong."

He took the pages and walked over to his desk. He flipped through them a few times. "Okay, so she's been in the news here and there."

Reid raised his eyebrows. "Here and there? She's left a trail of press releases."

Brent looked back down at the papers sitting in front of him. He quickly scanned the towns named in them. He blew out a short breath. "Okay, so she moves around a lot —no doubt about that." He looked at Reid, trying not to grin at his annoyed look, and then turned to Jac. "So, what's the issue here exactly?"

Jac threw up her hands. "I'm a little worried that Sandy is going to be alone with this person and Reid is being an idiot."

Brent smirked. "Not much new with that." He received a look from his partner and glare from Jac. Frowning, he looked over at the doctor. "Are you worried?"

She shook her head. "Not so much. But there is a lot of history I wasn't made aware of."

He wished now he'd gotten a coffee before coming down to the office. Scanning over the first few pages, he concentrated through the morning fog. She had been involved in leading police to a kidnapping site. Finding a murder weapon used in three killings. Locating an old cellar with trapped people, leading a family to a missing elderly relative. He flipped through a few more and looked up. "Miss Dante seems to be in the wrong place a lot." He looked at Jac chewing her lip. "What is this something that's nagging at you?" He pulled the priors sheet out of the pile and held it up. "She's never been convicted or guilty— just has really bad luck."

"Or is extremely lucky," Jac mumbled. Turning, she looked at Sandy. "When do you see her?"

Sandy glanced at the clock. "Two hours." She smiled at Jac. "I'll be fine; the judge just wants me to see if she's all right. He thinks it's more of a bored rich girl phenomenon really."

Brent gave her a puzzled look. "A what?"

Sandy perched on the edge of the desk. "She came from a wealthy family before she started moving all over the country. Sometimes children from a family like that will do just about anything to get noticed…"

Brent frowned at the papers in front of him. "That's a lot of *anything* she's been linked to Doc…"

"Exactly what I'm saying!" Jac glanced over at Reid, noting he still wasn't going to budge on the issue. "I wanted to wait outside Sandy's office while she's…"

"Absolutely not," Reid spoke quietly but knew he was heard when everyone turned to look at him. He studied Jacinda, and then glanced at Brent. "I don't want her near her. She's just barely recovered from the last criminal she got too close to."

Brent nodded and gave Jac a sympathetic look. "He has a point. If she is responsible for being involved in any of these – then you won't do much good being passed out on the floor."

Jac went over and dropped down into one of the chairs. "I know." She gave Reid a pouting look and shrugged her shoulders. "You're right."

Brent glanced from Jac to Reid and knew by the look on his partner's face those soft brown eyes were ripping him up inside. He couldn't blame him really. Maybe it was a male thing because he was also a real sucker for soft, pouting eyes

Reid shrugged. "Brent will go hang out in the Doc's office if it will make you feel better." She immediately smiled at him.

Brent's jaw dropped and he turned to look at the other man. "I will?" He looked over at the smirking doctor, then at Jac. She had turned those huge brown eyes on him. At that point he was sure they were boring right into his soul, pleading—he nodded. Sighing, he looked at the doc. "I guess I'm hanging out in your waiting room in two hours."

Sandy laughed. "I have very comfortable chairs."

"Lucky me." He watched Jacinda get up and go over and lean down and kiss Reid. Why did he feel like he'd just been sacrificed for his partner's good?

Sandy glanced at the clock. "Again, thank you for everything." She smiled at Brent. "I'll see you in a few hours."

He nodded, silently watching her walk from the room. Glancing back around he found Reid and Jac whispering face to face and shook his head. Picking up the papers, he started to read through them more thoroughly.

When Jac left to go to her own office, he turned to the man at the other desk. Reid grinned at him. He raised one eyebrow.

"Thanks," Reid said quietly.

Brent studied him for a moment. "What's really going on?"

"Jacinda was up half the night digging up stuff, something about all of it is really bothering her—when she starts to get that feeling, we both know there's something to it."

Brent held up the newspaper photo of a young girl with her parents. "I don't see *her* being a real problem."

Reid gave a helpless gesture with his hands. "I know, neither do I, but there's just something about it all that is really off."

He had to agree with him there, how was it this Felicity always seemed to be in the right place all the time? Things like that just didn't happen in his world. "You owe me one." He said holding out his empty cup.

Reid stood up grinning. "Yes, I do." He grabbed the cup and headed out the door.

"I want it in writing too." He mumbled only to be answered with a laugh.

Brent looked back down at the photo. He read through some of it … *Mr. Archibald Dante and his wife didn't wish to comment on why they're daughter hadn't been seen with them in over two years*… He studied the child in the photo again; she looked lost. What would cause her to give up her family and move to so many places? He read the date of the picture, briefly wondering what she'd look like all grown up. Great, now thanks to Jacinda his mind wouldn't shut up about it either.

3

Felicity got out of the cab, trying to fit all the bags into her small hands. It would have made more sense to pick everything up after your meeting she scolded herself. Managing to fit the last one onto her other hand, she bumped the door with her hip and then turned around to survey the building. *Oh, let there be an elevator.* It was bad enough she was ten minutes late, but she'd prefer not to arrive all out of breath and sweating. Taking a deep breath, she went into the building.

Brent glanced at the clock again. Maybe she wasn't going to show at all. He looked at the closed office door and debated on knocking, to ask Sandy what she thought, but as the door was closed, he figured she didn't want to be bothered. Glancing at the magazine table again, he rolled his eyes, there wasn't much there that appealed enough for him to even pick one up, never mind read.

The outer door flung open and in tripped a little blonde carrying as many bags as she probably weighed. He watched her struggle to close the door for a moment and was about to get up and help when half of what she was trying to hold slipped from her hands, scattering across the carpet.

Sighing loudly, she closed the door, now almost empty-handed. Turning around she looked at the notebooks and supplies all over the floor. She smirked at the man sitting in the waiting area. "That was rather graceful, wasn't it? Fall in the door and toss everything on the floor." Setting the rest of the bags on a chair, she knelt to start shoving things back into a bag.

Brent sat there for a moment. This was the woman that Jac didn't want the doc alone with? Snapping out of it, he got up and went over. Squatting down he began to pick up pencils and booklets that were scattered all over. She glanced up at him, the long wavy blonde hair half hiding her face, and smiled at him. The palest blue eyes he'd ever seen paralyzed his speech.

"Thank you." She flipped the hair out of her face and looked around to see if she'd missed anything. "I usually don't make such a dramatic entrance, really." She got back to her feet, setting the bags with the other ones on the chair.

Brent stood up and looked down at the tiny woman. Her appearance reminded him of a porcelain figurine. "No problem." He finally made his mouth say.

"Felicity?"

They both turned around to see Sandy standing at the door.

Felicity nodded. "Yes."

Sandy stepped back. "Come on in." She gave Brent a knowing look.

Felicity smiled at him again. "Feel free to draw something if you have the urge." She motioned to the bags on the chair and walked into the office.

He stood there staring at the door for a moment after it closed, then his brain kicked back in. *Well, you wondered what she looked like all grown up.* Very fine was all he could think at that moment. Sighing he went and sat back down. It only occurred to him at that moment that no one told him how long this appointment was supposed to be.

~

Felicity looked around the room before walking over to sit on the couch. Pulling one leg up under her body, she leaned on the arm of the couch and then smiled over at the other woman.

Sandy sat down in the chair across from her, glancing at the notebook that always sat beside her. She didn't think she'd really need it today; something told her that this woman was used to the routine as far as the private sessions went. "So, I'm Doctor Gains—Sandy." The smiling woman nodded her acknowledgment. "I've read all the reports, seen the newspaper clippings, so I know all that stuff." She paused for a moment and studied Miss Felicity Dante. "What I'd like is to hear is all from you—not some misconstrued reporters' version."

Felicity raised both eyebrows at her for a moment before recovering. "That's the first time I've heard that." She smirked. "Where is the how do you feel part?"

Sandy laughed. "Oh, I might use it at some point, but what I'd really like is the truth." She tapped the notebook beside her. "I have to report back to the judge that sent you here; it would be a lot easier to play his game if I'm on the same field with you."

Felicity nodded and then sat there thinking for a moment. She studied the doctor for a moment, many expressions crossing her face. "You may not like or believe the truth Doctor Gains."

Sandy pouted her lips out for a moment trying not to smirk. "You might be pleasantly shocked to see what I am capable of believing."

Felicity gave her a skeptical look. "I really don't know where to start."

"Let's start with the reason that brought you here to my office – then we'll go from there."

Felicity nodded slowly. "Okay." She looked down at the floor for a few seconds searching for the right words. "I see things. Inside my head . . . like you would on a tv screen I suppose." Chancing a glance at the doctor, she expected to see that academic look on her face. It wasn't, she was actually listening to her. "The things I see are things that are actually happening—at that moment to someone else." She leaned back on the couch, looking around for a few seconds, giving the doctor time to ask questions if she wanted. When silence met her, she continued. "I'm here because of something I saw. Stupidly, I panicked and ran to the police, hoping they would do something . . . anything to help."

"What did you see?"

Experience told her not to answer, but her mouth ignored her head and did anyways. "I saw a little boy, probably around seven or eight, and a little girl; I'd say she was four, if that." She took a calming breath before going on. "They were somewhere dark and hidden, I couldn't figure out where—they were scared and upset..." She remembered the little boy cradling the girl to calm her down so she would sleep. "They took the little girl, and I freaked out..."

"Who took her?"

Squeezing her eyes shut, she took a deep breath. "I don't know, it was dark and shadowed, I couldn't see."

"Where did they take her?"

Felicity sat forward shaking her head. "I don't know. I wasn't connected with her, just the little boy. He was scared and upset. He didn't want them to take her, then he just cried and cried..." She looked over at the doctor, who surprisingly was sitting forward in her chair as well as listening. "I felt lost and helpless— I wanted to help so I went to the police." She sat back. "And now I'm here and somewhere out there is a little boy alone, confined in the dark and I have no way to find him."

Sandy sat there, looking at her for a long moment. "You're connected with the little boy? Still?" She nodded. "How do you know these things are in the here and now?"

Felicity was actually shocked by the question. No one had ever asked in such a way that made her think they might believe her. "I just know. In the past I've found . . . people from my visions..." She took a deep breath. "But they were adults, and I could pick up much more that they noticed."

"The newspaper stories, the murder, the lost people, all the others— they were true?"

Felicity looked at her for a long time without answering. Her face said she was concerned, her body language said she had her entire attention. "Yes." She whispered it like it was a sin she was guilty of because to her it was – all the ones she'd never been able to help. "But there are so many I could never help."

"That's an awful thing to bear." Felicity just nodded at her. "When does this happen? Awake? Asleep?"

She cocked her head and studied the doctor cautiously. Was this where the hidden mockery began? "Awake, but I more or less become paralyzed when it happens, at least I think I do because I'm always exactly as I was beforehand."

Sandy frowned for a moment. "Do they physically affect you?"

"Uh - sometimes I'm disoriented or even ill, but other times just tired." It was an odd question for someone to ask, how would she know to ask it?

"Is the reason you move around so much because people have found out or is there another reason?"

Felicity was waiting to wake up and discover she was dreaming this entire time; these weren't the questions the doctors asked her. "Sometimes that's why." She looked at the floor and then back to the doctor. *You've come this far, might as well tell her the rest.* "Sometimes I have to leave because I can't do anything to help. If I go to the authorities with any of it, it gets me sent to places like your office and I only see things that are fairly close to where I am…" She hated saying it out loud. "So, if I leave, the visions stop and I don't have to sit and watch the news every night to see the outcome of the latest tragedy."

"Self-preservation." The Doctor whispered as she looked down at her own hands clenched in her lap.

"Sometimes it's the only way." She sat back, looking at the doctor.

The doctor sat there looking at her for a moment and then grinned. "Would you be entirely shocked if I told you I believed every word?"

Frowning, Felicity nodded at her. "Yes." *I'm dreaming, this sort of thing would never happen when I am awake.* She watched the doctor get up and walk over to her desk and lean as she wrote something down.

Sandy tore off the page and walked over. Sitting down on the couch next to her she turned. "This is going to come as a bit of a shock to you, but I do believe you, completely. I'll explain later on why I do." She smiled. "I'd like you to do something for me." Suspicious gray eyes studied her. "I'd like you to not pack up and leave just yet." She smirked at the surprised expression she received. "I saw the supplies in the bags you brought with you—you're planning on moving on soon, aren't you?"

Not sure at this point what was happening at all Felicity nodded slowly. "I was."

Sandy smiled. "Okay. Please don't, just yet." She held out the piece of paper. "I'd like you to meet me here at this address later." She glanced at the clock, wondering how much time she'd need to talk to Jac and calm Reid down. "Let's say around seven."

Felicity looked at the address. "It's not too far from where I'm staying."

Sandy grinned. "Good. That's my friend's address and she has a few things in common with you, but I'll explain all that later."

"She does?"

Sandy nodded again. "Yes, and I think we might be able to find a way to help that boy." She paused and wondered how calmly the detectives were going to take this. Probably not calm at all. "So, will you meet me there?"

Felicity sat there looking at her for a moment. She couldn't explain why, but the doctor was very convincing. Of course, it could be some kind of trap, but in as many ways as she could think, she couldn't see why the doctor would even bother going that far. "I can try to."

Sandy patted her leg twice lightly and stood up. "Great." She started walking towards the door. "Do you need a ride home?"

Felicity gave her a blank look. "I can take a cab."

"Oh, because I'm sure Brent out in the waiting area would drop you off and help carry all your purchases if you want."

Felicity stood up and started walking towards the door. "You want one of your patients to take me home?"

Sandy laughed, pausing with her hand on the doorknob. "He's not a patient; he's a friend that was waiting."

"Oh." She shook her head. "No, really I'll just take a cab, I have another stop to make."

Sandy nodded. "Okay then, I'll see you at seven."

Felicity nodded and walked out of the office. She walked out into the waiting area and tried organizing the bags before she tried to pick them up. That was the weirdest therapy session she'd ever experienced. She might actually show up later, just to see what happened next. The man in the waiting room stood beside her.

"Can I give you a hand with those?" Brent was quite happy he was speaking this time.

Felicity smiled and shook her head. "No, but thanks for offering." She stepped towards the door.

Brent moved over to the door and opened it for her. He reminded himself not to stand there and stare at her as she walked down the hallway. Closing the door, he turned around to see the doctor grinning at him. "It went all right?"

Sandy nodded. "More than all right." She looked at her watch. "Can you be at Jac's around six tonight? I may need help convincing Reid."

His eyebrows shot up. "I can be. Convincing Reid of what?"

She grinned. "I'll explain it all later. I have some work to finish so I can get there early enough to explain it all to Jac." She smiled again. "Thanks for watching out for me."
"No problem." He stood there after she'd closed the door, and then shook his head. He was supposed to go back to the office and tell Reid what? Nothing? Because from where he stood that's exactly what he knew, nothing.

4

As Brent raised his hand to knock, the door flew open. He studied the aggravated expression on his partner's face. "Guess this means you've been waiting for me?"

Reid stepped back and scowled. "Maybe now that you're here someone will tell us why we're having this meeting."

Brent thought it would be better if he didn't comment. Reid seemed more like his usual grouchy self. He saw the smirk on Jac's face that confirmed she knew he was a bit irritated, to say the least. He glanced over at the smirking doctor. "Well then, please put him out of his misery."

Sandy laughed as she went over to sit down. "I only wanted to have to try and explain this once."

Jac pointed to the other chair and grinned at Brent. "You were supposed to bring back inside information."

He sat down and shrugged. "Hard to do that when all I did was sit in a room, alone." He gave Sandy a serious look. "Now, what's going on?"

Sandy leaned forward in the chair. "I had quite the interesting session with Miss Dante." She paused for a moment like she wasn't sure how to begin this. "I've actually asked her to meet me here in about an hour." She smiled waiting for the reaction she knew was coming.

Reid held up his hand. "What do you mean here? Why?"

"I believe the four of us—actually the three of you can help her. I've already done my part in helping, by getting the judge off her back."

Jac gave her a curious look. "What did you do?"

Sandy clasped her hands in her lap and smiled. "I've told the judge that she has dreams and believes they are real—which isn't uncommon, and that I would be helping her through this."

Brent was getting more confused as they went. He studied the doctor for a moment. "And?"

Sandy shrugged. "She does have dreams, only they're real and she has them when she's awake."

Reid smirked. "What like a vision? Come on . . . and you believe this crap?"

Jac turned and glared at him. "Just sit there Reid." Her tone wasn't pleasant.

Brent covered his face for a moment, trying not to tell his partner out loud that he'd just walked himself into the doghouse. He glanced at Reid who clearly knew his mistake. Letting out a deep breath, he looked back at the doctor. "Why do you say they're real?"

Sandy turned from looking at Reid. She should have known he would be the most open to this. The man had accepted Jac's ability with nothing more than a 'wow'. "Felicity explained how she's been in so many right, but wrong places in her life. You have to admit that alone says there's something different going on."

Brent glanced at the scowl on his partner's face. He figured he'd better just do the talking this time. "So, she sees what's happening to others?"

Jac leaned forward again. "Does she know these people?"

Sandy thought for a moment. "I don't believe so." She smiled at her friend. "She also suffers after them sometimes—just as you do."

Brent watched Jac sit back and chew her lip. "Okay, if these dreams are real, I can see how Jac can help." He glanced at Reid for a moment then back to the doctor. "I've seen how she is after doing what she does, and she could help Miss Dante through that I suppose – but what do Reid and I have to do with it?"

Sandy glanced at Reid, then back to Brent. This was the part she wasn't sure how to explain the most. "The things she sees are happening— now— in this time." Jac sat silently looking at her. "When Jac sees things, they're in the past." Brent nodded. "The latest incidents of what Felicity has been seeing, and you'll have to confirm all this with her, is of a child, a little boy." Both men suddenly took on their detective expressions, listening to pick out the information. "Apparently there was a little girl as well, but someone took her, and now the little boy is alone in the dark..."

Brent leaned forward. "Who took her?"

Sandy shook her head. "I don't know the details. She wasn't connected with the girl child, but the boy and still is."

Reid stood up, putting his hands in his pockets. "Still is?" He looked at Brent to see if he was getting all this as he was.

Sandy nodded. "Really, you'll have to ask her about the details of it all I know is when she went to the police to get help for this child, she was sent to me."

Jac sighed. "I can relate to that." She glanced at Reid. "Of no one believing me enough to help someone."

Reid opened his mouth and then closed it again. He turned to Brent and studied him. Taking a deep breath, he looked back at the doctor. "If she knows details, we can look into it."

Sandy smiled. "I figured you would." She paused, looking back at Jac. "Would you pick up any of it if you touched her?"

Jac's eyes widened. "You want me to touch her and see what I can see?" Sandy shrugged. "Other than it being a bit of an invasion, I don't know if I want to..."

"I agree with that," Reid added in quickly. He looked at Jac for a long moment. "I don't think you being involved in this, in *any* way, is a good idea."

Jac chewed her lip. "Whether it is or not— isn't the point." She stood up and looked out the window. "If these dreams, visions, are real and I believe they are if Sandy thinks they are, then this woman has been going through most of what I have all my life." She glanced at Brent to see if he was following her point, he was. "She's been alone or an outcast, probably moving from place to place just to survive with some sort of serenity."

Sandy nodded. "She's right, Felicity was getting ready to move on, I asked her to just stay long enough to come here tonight."

So many pieces were falling into place for Brent. It made perfect sense now, why she'd leave her family, why she moved so often. Of course, the links of her being involved in so many crimes and scenes all made sense now too.

Brent leaned back in the chair and looked at the others. Jac was chewing her lip, Sandy sat waiting patiently and of course, Reid had that stubborn look on his face. Clearly, the man didn't understand he was standing on very thin, basically see-through thin, ice at this moment. He cleared his throat. "I vote we see if any of us can be of help at all." He watched Reid's face for signs of objections. Reid was too busy falling into Jac's soft pleading brown eyes. He glanced back at Sandy. "Does she know we're going to be here?"

Sandy shook her head. "I didn't want to scare her off."

He blew out a breath. "Well, she saw me today, but I don't think she would have been so cavalier if she'd known what I do."

Sandy nodded. "I know, and I don't know how to get around that."

Reid shrugged. "We'll just avoid it, for now, tell her when we need to."

Brent raised an eyebrow at him. "Which means you can't start interrogating her as soon as she walks in the door." Reid snarled at him. "Does she know about Jac?"

Sandy shook her head. "I thought it best to leave that up to Jac."

Jac bit her lip. "I suppose she would trust more easily if she knew about me." Sandy nodded. Jac sighed. "Okay, we'll start out with me and hope she will trust us after that."

Sandy smiled. "Okay then." She stood up and headed towards the kitchen. "I'm going to go make coffee."

~

Felicity stood across the street from the address she'd been given. *Getting pretty careless, aren't you?* She looked to both ends of the street again. Why had she agreed to come here? She didn't know what she was walking into— really didn't know anything about the Doctor. She leaned against the street post again and looked at the house. *Let's face it, you're in shock and curious at the same time.* The doctor actually looked and sounded like she'd believed every word. That's never happened – ever. Her own mother hadn't believed her, even when she said she did. Who was this friend of the doctors? What did she share in common with her? No one had anything in common with her, she knew this, she had searched through every means possible. But she had to know for sure. And if this went badly, what did it change? Nothing. She was still ready to move on.

Okay. Taking a deep breath, she started across the street towards the house. She clutched her bag to her side, making herself take those last few steps to the door.

The doctor opened the door, smiling at her as she invited her in. As the door closed behind her, she swallowed down the apprehension suddenly straightening her spine.

Sandy smiled. "I'm glad you decided to come, Felicity." She motioned towards the other room. "The friend I mentioned is waiting." She turned and led the way in. Motioning to Brent she grinned. "I'm sure you remember Brent from earlier today."

Brent stood up and walked over. He stopped and smiled, looking into her pretty blue eyes. He held out his hand. "Brent Jordan."

Felicity looked up at him for a moment then smiled. "Felicity Dante." She smirked. "That entrance wasn't quite the showstopper I managed earlier today."

"Did you make it home all right with all of that?"

"Yes, I managed to not throw it around again." She looked over at the couple standing close together behind the doctor. She offered a polite smile. "Hi." The lovely dark-haired woman smirked hesitantly.

"I'm Jacinda Brown." She touched the arm of the tall man standing beside her. "This is my boyfriend, Reid Merritt." He nodded politely at her.

Sandy motioned towards the chair. "Please sit down." She watched as she sat hesitantly on the edge of the chair. "I realize this is probably a bit odd for you."

Felicity laughed. "A bit?" She flipped her long hair back from her face. "This is the first time in my life someone has believed a word I've said, so you'll have to understand if I'm a bit on edge."

Sandy smiled at her. "We completely understand." She motioned towards Jac. "I'm fairly certain Jac understands exactly what you're feeling."

Jacinda sat towards the edge of the couch. "I have a hundred questions—but I think I should show you something first." She chewed her lip for a moment, looking down at her hands. "I also see things." The other woman's face showed nothing. "It's not the same as you, I have to touch something to see."

Felicity sat there for a moment digesting this. "What sort of something?"

Jac watched her eyes for those telltale signs of disbelief. "Something that can hold memories, vibrations. Wood, metal…"

"You see memories?"

"It's hard to explain really." She looked over at Reid for a moment then back to the woman. "Um, it would be easier to show you— than to explain."

Felicity sat there for a moment, silently wondering if she were in some sort of dream. "What do you need to show me?"

Jac got up slowly, going over, and sat on the edge of the table in front of Felicity. "Something personal, but please not embarrassing." She gave Brent a knowing look. He smirked.

Felicity nodded slowly. She didn't have much that she'd call personal really; she looked down at her hands. Spotting the bracelet, she always wore, she held up her hand. "My bracelet?"

Jacinda nodded at her. She took a deep breath and held out her hand.

Felicity undid the clasp and set it in the other woman's hand. Watching as she took deep breaths. Glancing around at the others, she noticed they were almost holding their breath waiting, the same as she was.

She watched a tear roll down Jacinda's cheek from beneath her closed lashes. And she knew. The brown eyes opened and looked at her. Felicity knew from the distraught expression that she really did know.

Jac swallowed. "Even though her son didn't make it – she still gave this to you?"

Felicity swallowed the lump in her throat. "Yes. She was just relieved to know." She accepted the bracelet back. "I wish I'd been able to find him sooner." Looking up from her wrist, she whispered. "The others that were trapped survived."

Jacinda stood up out of anyone's reach and held her palm over her stomach. Reid started to get up and she shook her head. "I'm fine, just a little queasy." She gave Felicity a shaky smile.

Felicity smiled back. "I can relate to that." She shrugged. "But usually I'm too disoriented; to feel nausea." The other woman nodded still focusing on breathing through the feeling. She looked over at the redheaded man. He wasn't paying attention to Jacinda; he was studying her instead. "Is the word freak going through your mind right now?" It wouldn't have surprised her if he'd said yes.

Brent shook his head. "No. It's more like wow, actually."

Felicity knew her jaw dropped; she honestly didn't know what to say.

Jac chuckled quietly. "It's a nice surprise, isn't it?"

Felicity nodded and looked around at the others. "I feel like I'm in a dream today and seriously I don't want to wake up."

Brent sat there for a few minutes, and then glanced at Reid a few times. He knew this would come out more pleasantly from himself than his partner. "Sandy told us about your latest . . . vision. About a boy?"

Felicity looked at him for a long silent moment. "You're a cop." It wasn't a question. Brent nodded. She looked over at the doctor. "I've been trying to figure out how all of this was going to help that child." She looked at Reid and smirked. "And you detective would be his partner," Jac smirked and nodded.

Reid gave her a puzzled look. "You read people too?"

Felicity shook her head. "No, you just look the part." Jac patted the frowning man's knee. Taking a deep breath, she looked back at the other man. "So, how exactly do you plan to help?"

Brent's brows drew together. "I'm not sure. Can you tell us about any of it?" He didn't know if these seeings or visions, stayed with her, maybe if they were gone as soon as she came back to—from— he had no idea as he seemed to have found himself in unfamiliar water again.

Felicity looked down at the floor. She could tell them, but who said they would believe her? She picked up the bag she'd tucked in behind her when she'd perched so cautiously on the edge of the chair. "I can show you what I've written down after the last few." She pulled the weathered notebook from her bag and flipped it open. Glancing up at them, not sure why she needed to explain, but did anyways. "I carry it because I never know when I'm going to see." She found the starting point to the visions with the little boy and girl and then held the book out to him. "I write it down as soon as I'm focused again, while it's all still fresh."

Brent took the book and glanced down at it. The handwriting was messy, but he still managed to read it. He read through the first page and then glanced up at her; she sat there watching him with a look of anticipation on her face. He looked back down again, skimming over the next few pages. It was quite detailed, giving him the time she saw things and the details of what she saw. Numbers were beside some of the entries. "The numbers are …" He continued to read.

"I can sketch fairly well, so I try to draw parts of what I've seen sometimes."

He looked up at her. He wondered if that was what all the paper and pencils she'd dropped had been for but decided that could be asked at a later date. "Do you have those with you?" She nodded reaching back into the large, faded bag. Pulling out an old folder, she handed it to him. He handed the notebook over to Reid and tried not to smile as Reid almost ripped it from his hand. He opened the folder and studied the first sketch. It didn't reveal anything he could follow, so he flipped through the next few. He looked back up at her again. "No people?"

She sighed. "No. It's probably the only thing on the planet I can't draw well enough to make them look real."

He pursed his lips and looked back down at the sketch. They were good, but without a face, he didn't know what they could do. He handed the folder over to Reid and sat back. "Can you remember what they look like?" She nodded. He waited for Reid to look up from the sketches. When he did look at him, he could tell without words that they were on the same wavelength. What she saw was real. The sketches were real. "Can you get Ricky in on this without alerting anyone— just yet?"

Reid rested his chin in hand for a moment and studied Brent.

Sandy cleared her throat. "I'd say my work here is done. I'm going to get going."

Felicity gave her a shocked look. "You're leaving?"

Sandy smiled. "Yes, the four of you will figure all of this out and after the last case I knew too much about, I've had my fill of police work."

Brent laughed. "We promise not to let Jac do anything she shouldn't. Now that we know what she shouldn't do."

Jac pouted when Reid nodded. "Fine, it will strictly be hands-off for me."

Sandy smirked at Jac's pun. "Make sure it is." She smiled down at Felicity as she stood up. "I'm sure I'll see you again soon."

Felicity lowered her head for a moment then offered a smile. "Thank you for everything."

5

Felicity watched the man behind the steering wheel. "Thanks for the ride home."

Brent smiled over at her. "No problem." He glanced back to the street. "Do you need to go anywhere else?"

She pressed her lips together for a moment and thought. "Actually, if it's not a problem, could we stop at the grocery store for a moment?" It still felt strange saying it out loud. "I'm always afraid to take a cab. With the visions back again, I'm afraid I'll phase out on some poor cab driver."

He found it odd that she thought of the driver before herself. "No problem." Turning his head, he grinned at her. "If you phase out on me, I'll just sit here and talk to myself until you're back."

She laughed. "Okay, but if it happens inside the store, just put me in a cart and get me out of there."

Brent frowned. "Does it happen often when you're out somewhere?"

"Not too often, then again I don't go out in public much." She shrugged. "Most people will just accept I'm not feeling well as the reason."

He glanced at her. "And those that don't?"

She shrugged. "I don't usually hang around afterward to ask their thoughts."

Brent turned into the parking lot. "So, you don't mind if I come in then?"

Felicity smirked. "No, actually it will be nice to know if it happens, someone there will know what's happening."

Parking the car, he took his time turning it off. He wasn't sure he knew what was happening. It hadn't been that long since he'd realized what Jac could do and now to be discussing visions like they were an everyday thing. *That's what you get for wishing for something different to happen.*

"Detective Jordan?"

He turned to see the curious look from the petite woman beside him. "Sorry, I'm still digesting all of this."

"I understand." She turned to get out of the car, waiting until he was out on the other side. "So, how long have you known about Jacinda?"

Locking the car, he stuffed the keys in his back pocket. "A few weeks."

She laughed. "No wonder you're still digesting." She smirked at him as they walked towards the entrance. "I guess we've taken your stable little reality and shook it up a bit."

"It needed some shaking." Brent followed her as she wandered slowly in the produce section.

She glanced up from the vegetables. "Jacinda helped with a case recently?"

He blew out a breath. "Yeah."

Setting the lettuce in the cart she asked quietly. "What does the department think of this?"

He smirked. "They think she's a brilliant researcher."

Pausing with the peppers in her hand, Felicity gave him a wide-eyed look. "They don't know?"

Brent shook his head. "Nope. Just Reid and I know." He shrugged. "It's easier that way."

She stood there studying him. Had she really been lucky enough to stumble on a few people that not only believed her but wouldn't expose her?

"Are you – okay?"

"Yes, just deep in thought." She pushed the cart a few more feet and then paused. "I'm not used to anyone knowing."

"I know." Brent watched her for a moment like he was trying to understand where her mind was. "We won't tell anyone if you're worried ..."

Dropping the oranges into the cart she interrupted him. "I'm not worried about that." Quickly she headed in the direction of the dairy section. He followed along behind her. She looked up at him as she pulled the cooler door open. "So, tomorrow when this Ricky comes to do the sketches, do I have to tell him anything?"

Brent shook his head quickly. "No. Ricky does a lot of work for Reid, never asks questions."

She frowned. "Why?"

His mouth quirked. "I never asked."

Laughing she turned the cart down the next aisle.

Brent watched her put several more items in the cart. "I'm going to make a guess, you're a vegetarian?"

"Wow, you are a good detective."

He grinned and stood up to his full height jokingly. "I try." Following her to the cash, trying to ignore the few men they'd passed leering at her as she breezed right by them. "So how do you support your vegetable habit?" He asked as he helped her put things on the counter. She didn't strike him as the type of person to live off wealthy parents. "I'm assuming you don't have any contact with your family ..." He didn't know how to word it, so he stopped.

Placing the last item on the counter, she gave him a hard look. "You assume correctly." Then she smirked. "If I tell you what I do to support my food habit, I might have to kill you."

Brent's eyebrows shot up. "Really?" He leaned down close to her. "I have my ways of finding out things."

Felicity laughed quietly. "I don't doubt it." She looked up at him for a moment. "You'll be the first person I've ever told."

He was silent for a few seconds. "You can trust me."

"I think I can." Studying him for a moment, then she glanced at the items the cashier was ringing through. "I'll be right back."

Brent watched her go over to the magazines. She bent down and pulled a small book off the bottom of the rack. Coming back over, she stopped right in front of him and held out the book.

He took it with a doubtful look, smirking she started putting the bags in the cart.

Looking back down at the book in hand. *A children's story? What did this have to do with anything?* He eyed her for a second, and then looked back at it. A rabbit and a squirrel, vaguely familiar, must have read it to one of his nieces recently. Looking at Felicity again, he gave her a puzzled look.

Felicity laughed as she paid the cashier. The lost expression on his face was the funniest thing she'd ever seen. Leaning towards him, she tapped the author's name on the book he held. When he looked up at her again, she pointed to her own chest. His eyes widened. Turning, she accepted the change from the clerk.

Brent looked at the book again and then tossed it on the counter. As he paid for it, he watched her pushing the cart to the entrance.

Walking quickly, he caught up to her. Opening the trunk of the car, he helped her put the bags in. She was still smirking.

Getting in the car, Brent turned to her and held the book up. "You're B. Woods?" She nodded but offered no comment. He looked at the book, again before setting it in the backseat. "That answers my next question." She lifted her eyebrows at him. He shrugged. "I've been trying to figure out how you moved around the country, without your parent's help or working in the public."

"That would be how." She said quite lazily.

"Huh." He knew it wasn't a very intelligent comment, but his brain was on overload from everything he'd been forcing it to take lately. He started the car. "Do you need to stop anywhere else?"

Felicity smiled. "No, that was it."

Brent nodded thoughtfully. "I'll get you home then." He drove in silence for the next few blocks. He kept glancing at her out of the corner of his eye. She'd been quiet since they left the store. "Do you want a ride to Jac's office in the morning?" He shrugged. "So you don't phase out on some poor cab driver?"

Felicity chuckled. "That would be great, thanks." She turned back and looked out the window. For the first time, she was not looking forward to the aloneness and safety of her little house. Today had been event-filled, and in a good way for a change. She turned to study the man driving in the dusk light. He had certainly accepted everything better than anyone she'd ever met. She smirked. Okay, the four people today that had believed her were the only people that had accepted everything.

Brent pulled the car into her small driveway. He noted she had no car. Then gave himself a mental smack, of course, she didn't have a car, how would she know when she could drive safely without phasing out or not? He turned the car off and reached for the door handle. "I'll give you a hand." Without waiting for a response, he climbed out of the car.

Felicity walked around to the back of the car. "Don't want me to toss the bags of food around?"

He grinned at her reminder of their first meeting. "We can't have you eating dented vegetables."

She chuckled as she opened the door, quickly setting the bags on the counter. Turning, she jumped when he was right behind her. "Oh, thanks."

Brent smirked. "I didn't mean to startle you."

"I'm not used to having anyone here, or really near me in any way I suppose."

He watched her, studying how quickly she was putting things away. "I'll get out of the way." She straightened and looked around at him quickly. "I'll see you in the morning."

Felicity leaned back against the counter. "Yes and thank you again, Detective."

Brent paused with his hand on the door handle. "Brent." Opening the door, he left quickly.

As he drove home, Brent thought about nothing but Felicity Dante. She hadn't been anything like he'd expected. He shook his head. He wasn't sure what he'd expected, but she definitely wasn't even close.

6

Felicity woke up with energy, for the first time in a long time. Her sleep hadn't been interrupted by any visions or the anguish following one that most time prevented her from relaxing and sleeping. Maybe it was from the fact that someone believed her—making her feel a lot less like a freak of nature.

She took her time getting ready for a change. It wasn't often she felt like taking special care of how she looked. Then again, how often did she have plans to actually speak to people? She paused in front of the tiny closet and thought. She couldn't remember the last time.

Selecting a long flowing dark blue skirt, she held it up to a white blouse. She shook her head. Just doing that gave her a flashback to her mother's endless lectures, when she'd been younger on dressing appropriately. Shrugging, she pulled the blouse out of the closet. Her mother hadn't been around for a long time to critique her selection of clothes.

Brent was just reaching to get out of the car when her front door opened. He dropped his hand and watched. She was smiling. He suddenly felt underdressed in his black jeans. But she looked just like a porcelain figurine in her dark skirt with a tight hugging top. The sunlight reflected through her long, pale hair as it hugged down passed her shoulders. When she looked at him through the windshield and smiled, he was glad he had a few seconds to compose himself before he'd have to speak.

Felicity climbed into the passenger seat and smiled over at the grinning detective. "Morning."

"Morning." He paused for another second to look at her, then turned and started the car.

He'd driven silently for several blocks. Felicity noticed him glancing at her a few times. She looked down at the folder of sketches on her lap. "After the sketches, what then?"

Brent stopped at the corner and briefly looked at her. "We'll run them with the missing children's database."

She pressed her lips together thoughtfully. "Oh. I check the websites quite often though…"

"They're rarely up to the minute." She gave him a puzzled look. He turned into the parking lot near Jac's building. "It's sad, but there are too many cases to keep the sites and networks up-to-date constantly." Parking the car, he turned toward her. "Ready?"

She looked around. "We're there already?"

"Yeah."

"Oh." She reached over and opened the door. "I'm just a bit nervous."

Brent climbed out and glanced at her over the roof. "Don't be, I'm sure you'll be just fine." He winked at her. "I'll sing and distract everyone if you phase out."

Laughing, she walked over to stand in front of him. Even with the heeled boots she had decided to wear, she still had to tip her head back to look up at him. "Please get someone to record it, so I can hear it later."

He cleared his throat. "Trust me; it's not anything you'd want to hear." Turning, he led the way into the building. Standing there looking down into her lustrous eyes had made him think of things he had no business thinking.

Jac got up from the table when they walked in. "Hi." She gave Brent a huge grin. "I knew you'd be gallant and pick Felicity up."

Brent grinned back at her. "Of course. I carried her groceries last night too."

Jac's eyebrows went up then she glanced at Felicity. She was laughing. Jac motioned them in. "Have a seat. Reid just ran out to get coffee, and Ricky is running a few minutes late." Felicity walked past her. Jac frowned. "Felicity, you're cheating."

Felicity turned and gave her a puzzled look. "I am?"

Jac grinned. "You wore heels. I liked that you were just as short as I was."

Felicity set the folder down and shrugged. "I felt like I was standing in a forest last night when the two detectives stood talking over my head."

Jac chuckled. "You get used to it."

Brent walked over and leaned against Jac's desk. He looked down at Felicity. "Hey, I'm the short one."

"Sure you are." She followed his eyes when he looked towards the door to see his partner coming through the door. Maybe he had a point. The larger man almost filled the doorway. She smirked at him. "So, did you two get kicked off a football team or something? Decided to scare and protect instead?"

Brent laughed at Reid's bewildered look. Taking the cup his partner held out he shrugged towards her. "Felicity thinks we're trees."

Reid smirked. "I'm just a little guy, my father was big."

Felicity stood there looking up at him.

Jacinda handed her a cup. "Regular, right?"

Felicity nodded and took the coffee. "Yes, thanks." She glared up at Reid, who she was sure was purposely standing at full height to make her feel very small. "Sit." She told him quietly.

Brent laughed as Reid gave her a peculiar look but sat down anyways. He waited for Jac to stop giggling. "What time is Ricky going to be here?" He had barely finished the question when someone knocked on the door.

"Now," Reid said in a bland tone.

Felicity looked at the door, then over to Brent. He winked at her, making her feel less anxious. "Don't forget you promised to sing."

He laughed, not even knowing where to begin to explain to his partner why he was singing.

~

Brent thanked Ricky as he walked out the door, and then turned to look at Felicity. She'd been sitting there holding the sketch of the boy for a few minutes now. He didn't have to ask if Ricky had captured him the way she'd seen him, the anguished look in her eyes told him the sketch was the boy in her visions. He walked over quietly when he realized both Jac and Reid were also watching her silently. Sitting in the small chair across from her, he clasped his hands on the table. "Would you like to come down to the station with us while we run these?" When the pained blue eyes looked at him suddenly over the sketch, he felt his heart stutter.

"Please," she said quietly. Taking the two sketches she quickly tucked them into the folder with her own. She wasn't sure she could stand just yet. Not once had she thought of how she'd feel to watch the little boy's face appear on the paper. The child that for some reason, she would never know or ever be able to explain was reaching out to her.

"We'll meet you down there," Reid said it quietly as Jac pulled him back towards the door. "Just lock the door on your way out, Brent."

Brent nodded without looking away from the trembling woman he sat across from. He waited until he heard the door close. "Are you all right?"

Felicity looked up from her hands pressing the folder closed. "Yes." Her voice vibrated with emotion. She cleared her throat. "It's just— I've never actually seen this child outside of my own head, I'm ..." She couldn't even describe the feelings she was having.

Brent reached over and placed his hand over hers. He felt the tremors going through her. He watched her look down at his hand. He wasn't sure what the expression was that crossed her face. "Let's go see if we can find out who this little guy is." She nodded abruptly.

Brent glanced up from the list he'd been reading. He checked to see if the women were still wandering back and forth in front of the computer. Looking at the pages in his hand he got up nonchalantly and walked over to Reid's desk. Waiting until his partner looked up at him, he held out the list. Reid looked at it then back up at him. Holding a finger over his lips Brent handed him the papers.

Reid frowned but took them.

Turning. Brent went over and stood by the computer. "It's going to take time ladies." He glanced back towards Reid. Obviously, by the irritated look on his partner's face, he'd read the list. "I'm going up to see if we can borrow a few minutes of Alec's time." Reid nodded. They both knew Alec McGowan had a passion when it came to missing children's cases. No one knew why exactly, but the fellow detective would go out of her way to get assigned any related cases.

Brent sighed as he walked slowly up the stairs. Personally, he wasn't fond of cases like this, the statistics for finding missing children were not favorable and he admitted— to himself only— that his heart couldn't take the ache that went with it.

Felicity sat and watched the faces flying by on the screen. So many young faces went across it. Were there really that many children out there with such uncertain futures? Glancing over at the tall detective, she noticed he still hadn't spoken a word in the whole time she'd been here. The only time he deviated from whatever it was he was working on was so he could follow Jacinda around the room with his eyes. Small pains of jealously stabbed at her a few times when she thought of how different Jacinda was from the norm and that she was able to find someone. Her mind was dying to know how that worked, with Jacinda picking up emotions when she touched someone, but common sense told her some things were better not being asked in front of a male. Shoes echoing on the stairs had her turn back towards the door to see Brent come meandering through the door in his easy way. She was surprised when a tall blonde followed him. Her jeans were faded, and her t-shirt tucked in to reveal a badge clipped to her belt.

Brent stopped just inside the door. "Felicity, this is detective McGowan. I've borrowed her for a bit to help us out."

Felicity stood up and tried not to notice how the other woman towered over her. She had to be at least six feet tall. She offered her hand. "Felicity Dante." The woman shook her hand briefly.

"Alec." She turned and nodded to Jac. "Hey."

Jacinda smiled and stood up. "Hi Alec, thanks for coming down."

Alec shrugged indifferently. "No problem, I was falling asleep over paperwork." Her eyes went to the monitor for a moment then to the sketch sitting on the desk. Flipping the long ponytail behind her she bent down and studied it. "You've seen him?"

Felicity walked over nodding. "Yes." She chanced a glance at Brent, not sure if she should explain. He just shook his head so she didn't say anything else.

Alec looked up at the screen as she spoke. "Good eye. It's shocking how many people don't realize what they see, or care to do anything about it."

Reid walked over and handed Alec the list he'd been studying. She took and glanced at it briefly before tossing it onto the desk. "You don't need to show me that Reid, I'm more than aware of that pathetic list."

Felicity stood there, not sure if she wanted to know what the list was. She looked over at Brent hoping for some insight then Alec sighed.

"Sorry, I get a little worked up when it comes to the missing kids." She blew out a long breath. "There isn't much that can be done until a match comes up though. Hopefully, a match comes up."

Felicity frowned. "What do you mean?"

Alec stuffed her hands into the pockets of her jeans. "Some people don't care. They should be shot, but regardless, they don't care enough to report it. Poverty-stricken families…"

Brent cleared his throat to get her attention. "I thought you could explain the statistics for Felicity, Alec. You know them by heart."

Alec nodded slowly. "Yeah, unfortunately." She looked back at the sketch on the desk before looking back at the others. "The sad reality is usually after forty-eight hours there isn't much we can do unless someone sees a particular child … and cares." She leaned back against the desk and crossed her arms in front of her. "In Canada and the US, there are over eight hundred thousand kids that go missing each year." She watched the shocked expressions cross over Jacinda and Felicity's faces. "I could break it down to how many kidnappings, parental abductions and go down the list, but I won't." She looked at the monitor again. "How long has this been running?"

Brent looked over at the clock. "A few hours."

She pursed her lips for a second before speaking. "You still have a bit of a wait then, it goes through the database from the longest to most recent."

Felicity sighed. "And there's no other way?"

Alec shook her head. "Not unless the parents come walking through that door to file a report." She pushed away from the desk and gave Brent a nod. "Let me know if you need any help once it comes up."

Brent nodded slowly. "Thanks, Alec."

Felicity watched her walk out of the office before turning back to Brent. "We just wait?"

Jac paced across the floor a few feet. "Do you have those journals and drawings with you?" Felicity nodded. "Can I see them? Maybe there's something that will give us an idea."

Reid put his arm around Jac's shoulder. "If anyone is going to pull something out of there, it will be you." He was rewarded with a stunning smile and a kiss on the cheek.

Brent chuckled and walked back over to his desk. "I'll make a few calls to the neighboring towns and see if anyone has reported anything while you ladies go through the journals." Jac was already looking through Felicity's notes before he even got to sit down.

7

Felicity sat there, trying not to ask questions and interrupt as Jac read through her notes. She'd tried hard to write down everything she saw, or hints of what she was seeing; it wasn't easy. When she snapped out of her frozen dreams, she was more often so disoriented that her hand would be shaking as she tried to write. She patiently sat there and watched as Jacinda started to glance through her sketches. "I wished I could draw people." She said quietly.

Jac smirked without looking up from the sketches. "Your sketches are a masterpiece in my opinion; I can't even draw a square or a straight line." She flipped through the sketches slowly, wishing she could just find one thing that stood out. They were good, very detailed. Turning the page, she stopped and stared at the next one. It was a lake, quiet and serene. Her nerves tingled. "There's something about this one…" She picked it up and then stood up, looking down at it.

Felicity stood and watched as she started to wander around the office, pausing every few feet and closing her eyes. She turned to notice both detectives had also stood up and were watching Jac very closely.

"There's just something in this one…"

Her face blanched as she stood there. Reid came around the desk quickly and stood beside her. He looked down at the sketch.

Pointing at the tiny dock on the far side of the lake, she glanced up at him. "It's the dock, isn't it?"

Brent was beside her in three strides and looked down at it. He noted the long weeds surrounding the well-drawn dock. Squinting he studied it again. Looking up at Reid he nodded. "I think it is."

"No." Reid shook his head and scowled. "She is not going there again."

Felicity looked from one to the other. "Where?"

Jacinda lowered her hand and looked up at Reid. "I don't have to go to the dock…"

"You're not going anywhere near there again."

Jac sighed. "Reid." She held up the picture. "It's a view from the other side of the lake, nowhere near the dock."

He looked at the sketch again and frowned. "Sorry, I jumped the gun."

Brent chuckled. "With good reason. I wouldn't have let her go near that dock again; I almost had a coronary the last time."

Felicity felt like she wasn't even in the room during this. "What is wrong with the dock?"

Jac looked over at her. "It was a murder site, and I got a little too close."

Reid snorted. "A little? You almost put yourself in a coma."

"Oh." Felicity clasped her hands in front of her. "So, you know where this lake is?" All three nodded. "We could go there and see if we can find the viewpoint for the sketch?" She took a shaky breath. "I'm pretty sure he was looking through a hole in a wall or through slats on a window." Reaching down, she flipped through the other sketches. "They're out of order…" She quickly found the sketch that went before the one they were looking at. "This is what I could see before he moved over and looked out at the lake."

Brent looked down at it. "Looks like a poorly boarded-up window." Reid looked over at it and nodded.

Felicity's heart was pounding. This was the closest she'd come to find out anything. They had a place to start. "I don't think they're still there, the room – it's different now."

Jac looked up at Reid for a moment. "If I could…" She didn't get a chance to finish what she was saying as the computer they'd all forgotten beeped.

Felicity turned quickly and looked at the screen. It had stopped on a picture that looked very much like the sketch of the boy. She moved aside as Brent came over and clicked on the file attached to it. The information came up on the screen. There was a name. Damian Stewart. She blinked. She knew his name.

Brent started the printing. He glanced over his shoulder in the direction where Reid had been standing. "Call the cap down and get Alec back in here."

Jac moved over to stand beside Felicity. She didn't have to touch the other woman to feel the anxiety and excitement going through her. She wasn't having the visions, but she felt a sadness mixed with anticipation coming from her.

Felicity looked at the screen again then at Jac. "How are they going to explain any of this?"

Jac shrugged. "Just follow whatever lead they give the Captain. He doesn't care about tiny details of how's, just the end results."

They both turned as the tall blonde detective came quickly through the door. She headed straight to the printer and picked up the sheets. "Three weeks." She flipped to the second page. "Two hours from here."

Brent straightened and walked towards her. On his way by Felicity, he touched her shoulder briefly, hoping she would take it as encouragement. He picked up her journal on his way and flipped it open. "Miss Dante saw him …" He glanced a Reid briefly. He had no idea how to explain the actual sighting, so he continued. "Two days ago."

Alec's eyes jerked over at her momentarily than to Brent. "Excellent. That's good news, increases the chances." She pulled a notepad out of her back pocket and began copying information down from the printouts. "I'll need a photocopy of the sketch; I want to take it to the parents and get some confirmation…" She paused and looked over at the two detectives. "Unless you have a problem with that?"

Brent smirked and put his hands in his pockets. "None. We're going to go back to where he was seen and have a look around."

Alec nodded and glanced at Jac. "Are you taking Jac?" She winked at the dark-haired woman. "I don't know what magic she has, but if anyone can find something it seems to be her thing."

Reid grinned. "You have no idea. But yes, we're taking her."

Everyone paused when the Captain came through the door. He noted Detective McGowan leaning over a desk writing and the picture on the screen. "Kidnapping?"

Brent shook his head. "We don't think so. A missing child." He motioned to the screen. "We made a match from a sketch." He paused when Alec held the pages out to the captain, then picked up the sketch and went to the copier.

Everyone watched as the captain read over the sheets. "Sighting recently?"

Jac smiled and walked toward him. "Two days ago." He smiled back at her. She motioned towards Felicity. "Captain Reely, this is Felicity Dante. She saw the boy."

Felicity walked over to the grinning man and extended her hand. "Hello."

The Captain looked at her for a moment as he held her hand. "A pleasure." Turning he zeroed in on Reid. "I don't want you barreling in on some parents and scaring the hell out of them, Reid."

Reid's jaw dropped briefly before he smirked. "That's why Alec is going to deal with the parents."

The Captain turned back toward the female detective. "Good." He watched Jacinda putting her jacket on. She stopped when she noticed him looking at her.

"We're going to go to where Felicity…" She didn't know how to explain it, so she turned to Brent.

Brent stifled a chuckle. "We're going to head over to where he was seen and take a look around."

The captain stood there for a moment then nodded. "Call in whomever you need."

Brent nodded abruptly. "Will do." Without waiting to see if the captain had more to say he went over and picked up the sketches and handed them and the journal to Felicity.

She didn't want to ask any questions or say anything that would delay this, so she quickly put her journal into her bag and picked up her jacket. Frowning she watched Brent start the search on the computer again.

"Just in case."

She nodded slowly.

Alec pulled the page out of the printer and headed to the door. "I'll let you know."

Jac turned towards Reid then stopped and looked at Felicity. She stood perfectly still. Her complexion was pale suddenly. Taking a few steps towards her she stopped and looked at her. "Brent." She whispered it. He turned around and then followed to where she was looking. "Don't touch her; I don't know if it would affect her."

He stepped closer and looked down at the motionless woman. Her skin looked pallid and little beads of sweat were forming across her forehead. He lowered his head and looked into her eyes. The pale blueness of them seemed to be darker and glazed over. He wanted to grab her and shake her out of it but remembered Jac's warning. The first question when she came back to them was to find out if touching her caused her distress.

Felicity took a deep breath and then blinked. Reid, Brent, and Jacinda all stood no more than a foot away looking at her.

She frowned for a moment. Letting out a slow breath. "It was blurry images, nothing I could pinpoint." She looked down for a moment before looking back up at them. "I think he was just groggy and waking up." She pulled out her journal and a pen. "I'll write on our way to the lake."

Brent hesitated after the others began to move. "Do you need a drink or anything?"

"No, I'm okay this time. Really." She pulled her jacket on. "The longer it is the harder it is on me."

He pulled his keys out of his pocket. "What happens if someone touches you during that?"

She shrugged. "I don't think anything. I know my parents tried to shake me out of it when I was younger, but it didn't do anything." She followed him towards the door. "Once I'm in there's nothing that can be done to stop it."

Jac gave Brent a worried look and then looked over at Felicity. "What if the person you're connected to, isn't well?"

Felicity looked down at the floor and studied an invisible spot. Memories flooded into her. "Then I don't fair well afterward."

Brent didn't like the sounds of that at all. He'd seen what afterward was like for Jac and it hadn't been good. At least Jac could prevent it, somewhat. Choose not to touch something or let go; but that wasn't the case for Felicity, she had no choice. "I think, if it were me, I'd be looking into a way to stop them somehow."

Felicity gave him a surprised look. "That's hard to do when no one believes your having them in the first place."

"Point taken." He motioned to the door and spoke over his shoulder to his partner. "We'll take two cars." He didn't wait for a response; just lead Felicity up the stairs.

Brent drove as she wrote. He knew when not to interrupt people, and most times it wasn't a hard thing for him. This time it wasn't the case. He had a hundred questions to ask the petite woman sitting beside him. When she closed the journal and put it back into her bag, he grinned over at her. "You weren't kidding when you said you phase out."

"I've been told I suddenly become a statue during."

"Whoever said it was right."

She looked out the window for a moment. She hadn't even asked where this lake was, so she didn't know how long the drive would be. "So, what happened at the dock in the sketch that you and your partner don't want Jac anywhere near it again?"

Brent let out a long breath. "A woman was murdered there, so Jac went to see if she could pick anything up." He raised his eyebrows. "Of course, at that point, we didn't even know what she could do." Felicity's eyes widened. "Exactly. She picked up the image of the killer and actually felt the emotions of the victim…" He shuddered. "She collapsed, we had no idea what was going on or what to do." He let out another long breath. "After we got her back to her place Sandy came flying in to take care of her." He stopped and studied her for a moment. "To be honest, I don't know how either of you women deals with this."

She felt her eyes burn and looked out the window so he couldn't see the watery look. "It's not easy," she whispered.

Brent studied her for a moment then reached over and picked up her hand. "It will be, now that you have others to help."

Felicity looked down at his big hand holding hers gently. "Thank you." She took a deep breath to try to curb the sudden weepiness that engulfed her. "It's been a long solo journey for me." She didn't move afraid he would release her hand. It felt too good, the contact of another to move away. There had been no one to hold her hand for her – ever.

"It's only a few minutes more." He said softly.

"I hope we can find something."

He glanced over at her for what he was sure was the fiftieth time since they'd gotten in the car. "I don't understand all the quirks of it just yet, but do you have a limit to the distance…" He really had no idea how to word what he was trying to ask.

"I don't know the exact distance; I just know it has to be relatively close for me to stay connected." She shrugged. "A few times, when things got to be unbearable for me . . . I had to leave. I packed up and got on a bus heading in what I'd hoped would be the furthest distance from where I was."

"Did it work? Did they stop?"

"It did, the times I picked the right direction at least." She smirked. "A few times I took myself closer, at least that's my guess because the visions would get stronger." She tried to block the memories of those times from her mind. Brent's phone rang, giving her the distraction she needed.

"Hello." He glanced in the mirror to Reid's car following him. "I think sticking together would be the best." He nodded. "Lead the way." He slowed the car down so Reid and Jac could pass them. "They have a map with any buildings on it."

"Oh." Felicity watched the car in front of them for a moment. "Do you and your partner do missing children cases?"

"We do whatever needs doing. Mostly the ones that no one else wants to go near – or can't figure out."

"I guess having Jacinda on your side helps."

"We've only had her for one, but so far yes."

"What is her official function at the station?"

He laughed. "Officially, as far as the Captain knows she does research only."

Felicity smiled. "I guess he's a need-to-know kind of man?"

"We only tell him what he needs to know if that's what you mean."

"Thank you for not telling him about me."

Brent glanced over at her before looking back out the windshield. "It's not my place to tell anyone, anything about you. That's your call completely." He reached over and squeezed her hand briefly before returning it to the steering wheel. "Maybe now you can stop running from one end of the planet to the other."

She hadn't even considered that in everything that had happened in the last few days. "I hadn't realized that possibility. I've been in a whole new experience zone in the last day or so."

He nodded slowly, understanding how different all of this must be to her. To finally have someone who knew, and someone who believed her. "What would you do if you stay?"

She pursed her lips in thought for a moment while watching the lake appear from out of the trees beside them. "Get a puppy."

"A puppy? That's it? You could finally set down roots and stay in one place and the first thing is a puppy?"

"I always wanted one, but didn't with all the moving around – buses, tiny spaces."

He laughed. "What kind of dog?"

"One that is all alone in this world, probably one that is too ugly for anyone to love it." *Like I've been for most of my life.*

Her comment told him everything. It told him she'd been alone and facing life and all the challenges it had forced on her without backup, without support in any way. He nodded to the car as it stopped. "Looks like we're here."

"I don't know whether to be happy or anxious."

Turning off the car, he pulled the keys out of the ignition and turned to her. "Just keep your eyes open and voice any thought that goes through your mind. Let Reid and I do the rest."

She took a deep breath and nodded. "Okay."

8

Felicity followed along silently as they walked beside the lake. There were only a handful of small cottages in this area. She looked across the lake at the dock on the other side. "We have to be close."

Brent took her elbow and steadied her over a rocky patch on the shore. "We're trying to find a building with the windows covered." She nodded and concentrated on not twisting her ankle and breaking it over the stones.

She sighed. "I'm not wearing the right footwear for doing detective work."

He continued to hold her arm lightly. "I'll do the detective part; you just continue to look good in those sexy boots." He winked at her.

"I'll do my best." They almost walked into the couple that had stopped in front of them. Turning, she looked through the dense trees off the shore. There was a small building there, she wasn't sure if it was a cottage or had been some sort of storage building at some point. She looked over at the dock. It was the same angle from her sketch. "That has to be it." Brent nodded without speaking.

Reid pulled gloves out of his pocket and held them out to Jac. "Put these on, until we take a look inside." Jac took the gloves and nodded.

Brent started walking towards the building. "You ladies stay right here and duck behind that log while we go have a look-see." He waited until Reid was right beside him then nodded to the right of the building.

Felicity moved over beside Jac who had moved immediately behind a large dried-out log on the shore. Her breath was caught in her throat as she watched the two men separate. Brent had moved his hand to hover inside his jacket. She knew he held it close and ready near his weapon. She held her breath when he pulled a flashlight out of his back pocket and grasped it in his big hand. He paused at the one corner of the small building and nodded over to his partner before moving around out of her sight. Losing all sense of time, she sat squatted there beside the other woman, who also hadn't said a word. There was no motion or sound coming from the direction the two men had gone. She looked at Jac and then back towards the trees. "I'm going to fall to pieces shortly if they don't come back."

Jac nodded quickly. "Me too." She nodded to the trees.

Turning her head quickly she saw Brent appear from the other side of the building. He motioned to them telling them it was okay to come over now. Trying to quickly follow Jac, without breaking an ankle she breathlessly reached the building and then stopped. Walking over slowly she touched the boards covering an opening. Turning she squatted down and looked towards the lake. "He was here." She whispered it more to herself than anyone.

Brent stood there and looked down at her. He couldn't imagine seeing something for real that you'd only seen inside your mind. Reaching down he lightly held her arm to help her back up. He pulled a camera out of his pocket and held it towards her. "We're going to take a look inside; can you take a picture of anything you saw in your vision?" She nodded and took the camera.

Jac stood there for a moment and watched Felicity snap the camera a few times before moving around the corner of the building. She looked down at the gloves on her hand.

Leaving the gloves on her hands she went around the opposite corner Felicity had gone.

Felicity stood outside the crooked, decaying door. She waited for the men to come back out. She could hear Brent talking on his phone. He was asking for a team to come and check the place for prints. Jac stopped beside her. She leaned over and whispered softly. "How much trouble would they be in with us here?"

Jac shrugged. "Not as much as I'm going to be in a few moments." She looked suggestively down at the gloves on her hands.

Felicity raised her eyebrows. She knew she shouldn't agree to Jac putting herself into harm's way for her. If it were only her she would have squealed to the men like a tattletale, but Damian— there was Damian. "I'll run interference." She whispered. Then straightened quickly when she realized Brent was standing in the small doorway, looking larger due to his size.

He gave them both a curious look. "They're long gone— By at least a few days, maybe more." He nodded towards the camera Felicity held. "Take as many as you like but try not to touch too much." Looking at the gloves on Jac's hands he didn't say another word only stepped aside to let the two women go inside.

Felicity stopped as she stepped through the door. The room was small. At one time it may have been white walls, but now they were a faded yellow with dark streaks of age covering them. Cobwebs filled each corner. A small old metal-legged table and two faded cracked chairs sat in the corner across from a small stove of some sort. She looked at the line hanging from the wall and realized it had been a long time since any power had been inside this building. Reid stood in the corner writing in a notebook.

Walking slowly over towards the curtained door, she stopped and hesitated before reaching with a shaky hand to lift the curtain out of her way. Brent moved to stand beside her and shine a flashlight into the small space. At one time it may have been a tiny space for a cot to sleep. An old blanket lay in the corner. She covered her mouth and nose with her hand, the dust covering the floor made her nose itch. Lifting the camera with a vibrating hand she took a picture of the blanket in the corner and then squatted down and snapped the camera at the boards covering a small broken window. Moving slowly towards it, she tried not to reach out and steady her trembling legs. When she reached the window, she crouched down and looked out the space between two boards. It was the place that Damian had looked out, she was sure of it. Moving her face back, she lifted the camera up and snapped it twice.

Standing, she walked over and stood looking down at the blanket. She wanted to pick it up and hug it as she knew Damian would have. She took an unsteady breath and looked over at Brent, who still stood in the doorway shining the light into the area for her. "He was here." She cleared her throat and frowned. "Could I just have a moment?" He nodded and reached out handing her the light.

When the curtain dropped back into place she knelt and looked around the tiny space. She snapped a few pictures of the darkened corners she had seen before. She took one of the curtains covering the door and remembered how Damian had stared at it, waiting. The curtain moved a bit and she looked at Jac glancing in at her. She shook her head. In here wasn't where they needed to see, they needed to know where he was going. Jac dropped the curtain back down. Taking a deep breath, she went back out through the curtain and looked around the filth of the room again.

The one chair beside the table had been cleaned recently wiped off if the second dust-covered chair was any indication. The top of the table was also dust free. She moved over and looked down at it. Looking up she noticed Jac was watching her every move. She grimaced and then went over and handed Brent the camera. "I think I got them all." He nodded and put the camera back in his pocket.

Reid's phone rang breaking the silence in the crowded space. He pulled it out of his pocket and headed back outside as he spoke.

Felicity looked back at Brent. She knew Jac wanted a minute alone in here, but had no idea how to possibly accomplish that. Flipping her hair back, she looked over at the curtain again.

Reid stuck his head in the door. "They'll be here in five."

Brent nodded. "Better meet them at the car."

Jac walked towards the door. "We're right behind you; I'll help Felicity navigate back there in her boots."

He nodded abruptly and went out the door behind his partner.

Felicity turned back to Jac. "Now or never?"

"Exactly." She pulled the gloves off her hands and then nodded to the table. "I just need to see what the person that sat there was thinking." She went over to the table and took a few deep breaths. "Don't touch me while I do this."

Felicity nodded nervously and looked back at the door. "Just try not to pass out and leave me here to explain by myself." Jac nodded but didn't speak again. She stood there and watched as she took deep breaths and touched the edge of the table, as you would if you'd been sitting at it. She took a sudden step towards her when Jac sucked in a breath. She sounded like she was in pain. "Jacinda?" She whispered it, not knowing if she should speak as well as not touch her. She watched Jac's knees pop like she was going to collapse and quickly looked back towards the doorway. *Oh, do I call for help?* She moved closer and hovered nearer to the woman that was panting now. At least I can try to prevent her from falling and completely messing up prints and things. She clenched her jaw and waited, hoping Jac would stop soon.

Brent stood beside Reid along the shore watching where they had parked the cars. Rubbing the back of his neck he glanced back towards the trees. He still didn't see the women. His gut clenched. "Reid."

Reid turned his head to look at him and then towards the path they had just come from. "Shit!" He took off running back towards the cabin.

They reached the door at the same time and Brent stepped through quickly and assessed the situation immediately. Cursing under his breath he stepped over and pulled Felicity away from Jac. Reid wasn't cursing silently as he pulled his jacket over his hands and grasped Jac under the arms to pull her free from the table. She slumped back against him and breathed in long deep breaths.

"Sick." She gasped.

Reid swung her up into his arms and headed out the door quickly with her.

Brent straightened and looked down at the guilty woman beside him. She looked up at him with wide eyes.

"I didn't know." She said it quietly. "I wouldn't have let her if I'd known."

He took her arm gently and headed towards the door. "She would have, whether you tried to stop her or not." Heading around the side of the tiny shack he stopped and listened. Looking around her, he spotted Reid leaning over Jac twenty feet into the trees. At least his partner had gotten her as far away from the scene as possible. He released Felicity's arm and stood there listening to the retching coming from the direction of the two on the ground. "She needs those salt things?" Reid held up his hand waving the black case. Of course, he was a step ahead this time. He glanced at his watch and then called out again. "We have to get her to the car before they get here."

Reid straightened a bit and looked towards them. "Head that way, I'll bring her as soon as I'm sure she's finished."

Brent glanced down at the concerned woman beside him. "He's going to be pissed."

Felicity looked away from him and turned towards the path. "Is she going to be all right?"

Brent shrugged. "I have no idea. This is all still very new for me."

Felicity stood beside the car and watched as Brent went to help guide his partner across the rocky ground. Jac was huddled into his arms, resting her head on his shoulder. When they got closer she moved around and opened the back door to Reid's car. She stood out of the way as Reid gently lowered her into the back seat. When he straightened, she touched his arm gently. "I'm sorry. I had no idea."

He looked down at her hand for a moment then sighed. "It's not your fault." He glared at the woman in the back seat. "I'm buying her gloves that lock around her wrists or something…"

"Shhh!" Jac panted and then breathed out slowly. "Shut up and listen." She took a few more breaths. "I'm going to …" She swallowed and paused. "Pass out. There's been more than one."

Brent looked at her then at Reid. "More than one child there, Jac?" She nodded, at least he was fairly certain the motion she made was a nod. He looked up when he heard the sound of tires on the gravel. "Team's here."

Reid looked in at Jac, then towards the two cars pulling in. He looked at her for a few more seconds, then leaned down and whispered. "Felicity is going to stay here with you while we get them started."

Felicity waited for him to back up, then slide in the back seat with her. She looked at the woman slumping with her head back, eyes closed as she took deep breaths. Giving Brent a hesitant look, guilt went through her. "Is there anything I should do?"

He shrugged. "There's water in my car in the back, see if you can get her to drink until we can get her to her tea shortly."

Jac took another breath. "No tea."

He chuckled. "You just take a nap and we'll have you home in no time." He straightened and closed the door.

Felicity watched them walk over to the others climbing from the cars. Reaching over she cracked the window a little bit. "You almost got me into a lot of trouble."

Jac smiled sleepily. "Sorry." She let her head drop comfortably to the side. "Had to. Tell you later."

Felicity waited to see if she said anymore, then realized she was sleeping. Letting out a long breath she leaned her head back and watched out the window. *Hang on Damian, we will find you.* She wished she had the ability to send that thought to him. To give him a little bit of hope.

As quietly as she could manage, she got out of the car and went over to Brent's.

Rummaging around in the back seat, she uncovered a case of bottles of water buried on the floor with blankets, a hat, and a pair of shoes. Apparently, the man was prepared for anything. She looked back towards the path leading to the small cabin; Reid was walking back towards her quickly. She went back over to his car and looked in at Jacinda. She was still sleeping and from the lack of expression on her face, she was sleeping very soundlessly. She stood there waiting for him to get closer.

"We're going to take Jac home and Brent will follow us shortly."

She nodded and quickly went over to get her bag out of the other car. "I'll sit in the back."

Reid nodded as he looked in the car at Jacinda. Felicity could see the concern on his face, mixed with frustration. She placed a hand on his arm. "I'm sure she's going to be fine."

He sighed. "She shouldn't have done that."

"What would you do?" She looked in at the sleeping woman again. "If you had the ability to do something, with any of your cases, what would you do detective?"

The frustrated man looked at her for a long moment. "Honestly? I don't know if I could be as strong as she is or you for that matter." He opened the front door. "Until a few weeks ago I dealt in facts—there was nothing else."

She smirked at him over the roof. "Then you'd better fasten your seat belt, I think you're in for a bumpy ride."

He grinned and got in the car shaking his head. He adjusted the mirror so he could see Jac easily as he drove. As he put the car into reverse, he glanced over to see Brent walking quickly towards the cars. He waved his hand in a circular motion telling Reid to get going, he was right behind him.

Felicity rode silently as he drove. She glanced behind them a few times to see Brent following very closely. She took a deep breath and then let it out slowly. Her whole world had changed so much in the last few days. Changes, she was more than used to. Moving as often as she had did that to a person. These changes though were something entirely different. For the first time in her life, she felt hope. She also felt a little less like some sort of freak. She thought back to the discussion she'd had on the way to the lake. Could she dream of staying in one place? Looking over at Jac, who was still sleeping, she smiled. She could stay here; nothing would make her happier. Hadn't she spent her entire life wishing for a friend or two? Someone she could call and just talk to? She wanted to reach over and run her hand over Jac's forehead, she looked cool, but until she knew when she could or couldn't touch her, she decided against it.

Reid held Jac's purse over the seat. "Can you dig in this bottomless pit and see if you can find her house keys?"

Felicity smirked as she took the bag.

9

Brent leaned against the doorframe of Jac's small kitchen. Felicity was rummaging around in the fridge. He noticed the pan on the stove. "Foraging?"

She bolted up and turned around. "I almost jumped in the fridge." He smirked at her. "I thought I'd put something that resembled food together for us." She looked towards the living room. "You don't think Jacinda will mind, do you?"

He crossed his arms loosely in front of him and shook his head. "No, she won't. After Reid holds her down and pours more tea into her, she'll have some oatmeal to settle her stomach."

Felicity wrinkled up her nose. "Can't blame her, have you smelled that tea?" He shook his head. "You don't want to, trust me." She waved a hand towards the stove. "I'm afraid I don't even know how to cook anything with meat, so hopefully the soup and tray I'm making will be all right."

"Have you never eaten meat?"

She turned to cut up the cheese. "When I was a child. The doctors had me try no meat, they believed maybe it was contributing to my ..." She smirked at him. "Episodes. It's very hard to go back to eating it when you've been without it. The taste and texture is..."

"Eww?" He offered with a smirk.

"Close enough." She set the cheese on the tray and moved over to the stove and picked up the lid to stir. "You don't notice the grease until you haven't had it for a long time." Picking up the lid again, she dropped it quickly on the pot. Shaking her hand, she looked down.

Brent was behind her taking her hand to look down at it. He turned her smaller hand over in his own; she'd burned the side of her thumb. Without releasing her hand, he moved over to the sink and turned the water on. He held her hand under the cold water. "Better?" She nodded. His head was bent down beside hers; he tried not to inhale the subtle scent she wore. It went straight to places he shouldn't be thinking about in Jacinda's kitchen.

Turning more towards him, she smiled up at him. "Thank you."

He flipped the tap off and handed her the towel sitting on the counter. Handing it to her, he should have stepped back; he knew this. Of course, he rarely listened to that little voice that told him what he should do and took her hand to hold it in his and check the burn.

"You must think I'm a bit of a klutz. The first time we met I fell in the door and threw everything on the floor and now I can't heat soup without injury." She looked up at him.

Shrugging, he stood there and continued to hold her hand. "I think you're a lady with entirely too much on her mind."

Felicity's eyes moved over his face, taking in the smooth lines. They stopped on his green eyes. "You have very pretty eyes." She said it softly.

Leaning his free hand against the counter, he leaned down trying to bridge the height difference. "I think that's supposed to be my line."

She smiled. "I've never been very good at following guidelines." Their faces were only a few inches apart at this point.

"No?"

His voice had dropped to a whisper. She looked into his eyes to see a playful suggestion. "No. Not at all." She stood her ground and refused to be the one to look away.

He moved his face even closer, not looking away from the sparkling blue eyes. "I'd like to explore this…" He watched her tongue dart out and lick her lower lip. He wanted. "Conversation - further. But Sandy just flew through the door and we're all about to catch hell for letting Jac do what she did." He straightened up and looked down at her hand again. "I'll go see if Jac has any burn ointment." He smiled when she just nodded at him.

Felicity continued to stand and lean against the sink for a moment. Her hand didn't even hurt; presently she didn't care if she had a hand. Her hormones had kicked into overdrive, and she wanted to whimper. Letting out a slow breath, she moved back over to the stove and turned the burner off. Shaking her head to clear it, she started opening cupboards to find bowls.

Carrying the tray out, she set it on the table and glanced over to see Sandy sitting on the edge of the couch looking worried. Standing there, she waited until they looked over. "I made some soup." She grinned at Jac. "I've put the water on for oatmeal."

Jac almost looked relieved about the interruption. "Thanks." She looked from Reid and then back to Sandy. "Go eat."

Sandy got up and walked over to the table. She shook her head and then sighed. Smirking at Felicity she sat down. "I can't even yell at you, because you don't know any better."

Felicity laughed. "If it would make you feel better Doctor, go right ahead and yell at me."

Sandy looked at her for a moment, pleased she'd settled into this odd little group of her favorite people so well. "I can't yell at someone with such fabulous taste in footwear." They both looked down at her boots.

Felicity shrugged. "Saved by my boots, I'll have to remember that." She motioned to Brent. "Sit, I'll just go get the oatmeal ready."

Reid sat beside Jac on the couch. They both watched Felicity come in and sit down. Jac leaned against him. "Thanks for feeding everyone, it's harder for them to yell at me if their mouths are full."

Felicity laughed softly. "I was just trying to feel useful. It's too bad Sandy had to leave before she finished."

Jac grinned. "I didn't realize she'd been called to begin with. She probably ran out in the middle of a session."

Felicity folded one leg underneath her body. "Are you feeling up to telling us now? I've been going out of my mind trying to decipher what you said."

Jac took a few slow breaths. "I think I can manage to fill in the blanks before I have another nap."

Brent perched on the edge of the chair. "You said there's been more than one?"

Jac nodded. "Yes, the person that was there with the boy – he'd been there before and was tired of being the one to have to sit in that crappy little shack with them during phase one."

Felicity looked from one detective to the other. "Phase one?" Her heart thudded in her chest. "Like the first step to a process?"

Reid got up and moved away from Jac. "This is a ring." He spoke to himself. Brent nodded.

Felicity leaned forward and regarded them. "A ring?" She looked at Jacinda for an explanation.

She just closed her eyes and leaned her head back. "He was thinking of the money, it was the only reason he put up with it." She opened her eyes and looked at Reid. "He was mad that he didn't get to stay at the hotel with them each time. He wondered if they could find a new location for him, he was tired of two nights without power…"

Brent pulled out his notebook and started writing things down. "Any idea of where the hotel was? Did he think about it at all?"

Jac closed her eyes and thought for a moment. "He couldn't wait to dump him off at Dusty's ..." She huffed out a breath. "That's as far as I got before Reid grabbed me." She gave Felicity an apologetic look. "I'm sorry."

Felicity slid to the edge of the chair. "Don't be. You have far more than I possibly could have come up with." She put her hand on her chest to steady herself.

Brent stopped and looked at Reid. "We need to get down to the station. Find out the owner of that shack. Do a run on any motel in a two-hundred-mile radius that has dusty in the name."

Reid nodded and pulled out his phone. "Find out exactly where the boy was taken from; see how far it is from the cabin. See if they picked up any prints. I have to call Alec and see where she is, we're going to need her in on this to run possibilities through." He wandered from the room while he dialed the phone.

Felicity was shocked they came up with all of that from the few things that Jac had just told them. She stood up and placed a hand on Brent's arm. "Do you think this a kidnapping ring of some sort?"

He stopped writing and looked at her. "It's looking like it." He put the notebook into his pocket. "We have a better chance of tracking them if this is something they've done more than once." He looked over at Jac, who was nodding off again. "Can you stay here with Jac so we can get down to the station and get going on this?"

She nodded. "So what are you going to do?"

"See if we can find this Dusty's – then we're going on a field trip."

"Oh."

He squeezed her hand before stepping over to his jacket. "We'll be back in a while; Reid isn't going to leave her for too long." He ducked his head into the kitchen to see if Reid was still on the phone. "If you see anything else, call." He pulled a card out of his pocket and wrote on the back of it. Handing it to her, he went out the door.

Felicity stood there for a moment before Reid came flying out of the kitchen. He looked around for a second and then looked at the door. "He went to the station." He frowned. "Go. I'll stay with Jacinda until you can get back here."

"Thanks." Going over to the couch he leaned down and placed a kiss on her forehead. "See if you can trick some more tea into her if she wakes up." He headed towards the door and paused with his hand on the handle. "I don't know if she has them every time, but there might be nightmares."

Felicity sighed. "Nightmares are something I know too much about." She offered him an encouraging smile. "Go, I'll call if I need to." She waved the card Brent had given her and watched him go flying out the door as his partner had done.

~

Brent looked up briefly as Reid walked in. "Felicity, stay with Jac?"

Reid nodded. "What do have so far?"

Brent sat back. "Alec will be back shortly. We're waiting on prints and confirmation of the owner of the shack." He motioned towards the computer. "I'm just running the name of the motel now."

Reid came over and looked over his shoulder at the screen. "Fifty hits. How far away are they?"

Brent glanced at the screen. "They have to be reasonably close still." Reid gave him a puzzled look. "Felicity said she can get on a bus and get out of range of them – so there is a distance involved."

Reid leaned his hip against the desk. "So you're thinking they just circle around the same area, moving locations often until the deals are final?"

Brent shrugged. "It sounds plausible at this point." He leaned back in the chair and studied his partner. "First thing you're not going to like is we have to talk to the Captain."

Reid grinned. "I can deal with that. What do you mean first, what else aren't I going to like?"

Brent sighed. "We're going to need Jac's help."

Reid scowled. "Not just for research?" Brent shook his head. Reid straightened off the desk and glared out the window. "As a last resort."

"Agreed." Brent glanced at the clock. "How open do you think Alec is?"

Reid spun around and gave him a puzzled look. "Open to what exactly?"

Brent rubbed the bridge of his nose. "To cluing her in on everything."

Reid hissed. "That's not our call."

"No, I know it's not. I think we should talk to Jac and Felicity about it though. The more help the better and we're not going to be able to snowball over the details with Alec for too long."

Reid turned and looked at the door. "We'll leave it up to them." He smirked. "Personally, I'd be happier if everyone here thought we were just damn good instead of exposing Jac."

Brent leaned back to the keyboard. "We are damn good. Go fill the captain in and see if we can get clearance for a road trip."

Reid nodded and went out the door again.

~

Felicity looked up from the book she was trying to focus on reading as Jac sighed. She smiled over at her. "Hi."

Jac wiped a hand over her face. "How long have I been out?"

"A few hours."

"Wow, I didn't think that little trip would take that much out of me."

Felicity set the book down and stood up. "How are you feeling?"

Jac sat up slowly. "Not too bad actually." She looked around. "What did I miss?"

Felicity sighed. "They flew out the door and I haven't heard a word."

"Really?" She stood up slowly, testing her legs. "I don't know about you, but I'm not one for sitting and being patient."

Felicity laughed. "Yeah, it's not one of my strengths either."

Jac nodded. "Okay then. Let me go splash my face a bit and then I'll see if I can find out anything for us."

"Please."

Jac set the phone down and turned to look at Felicity. "They're digging and organizing."

Felicity raised her eyebrows. "Organizing what?"

Jac shrugged. "I don't know. I was told not to worry about it and get some rest – they might be a few hours yet." She pursed her lips together. "Do you drive?" Felicity shook her head. "Right, I guess you shouldn't. I shouldn't right now either."

Felicity grinned. "I'll split the cost of a cab with you though."

Grinning Jac picked up the phone

Brent and Reid were leaning over a map when they walked into the office. Reid straightened up and went quickly over to Jac. "Why aren't you at home resting?"

She glared up at him. "I did." She stood with both of her hands on her hips.

"You shouldn't be out running around."

She raised her eyebrows. "Really?"

He opened his mouth, and then shut it quickly. "I just don't want you to overdo it."

Jac sighed. "I'm fine, really." She reached up and touched his face.

Felicity had moved over to stand beside Brent. She tried to look anywhere but at the couple now making sappy faces at each other. Looking up at Brent she smiled. "Hi."

He chuckled and grinned back at her. "Hi."

She looked at the map. "So, what's happening here?"

Brent handed her the list of motels and motioned toward the map. "We're planning a road trip."

She read the list and then looked at the map. "I love road trips."

Glancing over his shoulder at Reid coaxing Jac to sit down, he turned back and grinned at her. "I'm glad because I think I'll take you so I have someone to talk to when they start."

"Excellent." She looked over at the frustrated-looking woman who was trying really hard not to yell at the over-concerned man. "We're going on a road trip, Jac." She ignored the frown Reid gave her. Smirking she looked back up at Brent. "When do we leave?"

"We'll head out first thing in the morning." He looked over at the couple talking quietly. "The captain is clearing the way for us, Alec is going to stay here and do any running we need done."

"I have a fax machine and portable … everything, so we can have a traveling office if needed."

"I'm not sure what a portable everything is, but we'll take it." He rubbed his jaw. "I'm not sure if we're taking one or two cars at this point though, so try to keep it down to the bare minimum."

She laughed. "Detective Jordan, I may be the only person that can fit an entire household in a few bags."

"Oh yeah, I forgot." He looked over at the two that were now more in the corner than they had been. "Let me finish up a few details here, and then I'll give you a lift home."

She nodded and looked down at the map again. "Take your time."

10

Felicity paced around her small house in the morning. It hadn't taken her long to pack the night before. Packing quickly and going on the road was something she could do without thinking. She paused to check the bags again. Her printer and the fax machine were in one small portable case and her laptop in another. She had no idea what clothes to take for something like this, so she took mostly comfortable ones. She checked her watch again. Was it the trip that was making her so jumpy or the fact that she hadn't had any glimpses from Damian? Had they moved him further away? Lost in thought she jumped when someone knocked on the door. Moving quickly, she opened it to see Brent standing there grinning at her.

"Morning."

She smiled. "Morning."

"Ready to go?" She nodded. "We decided on two cars, we'll meet Reid and Jac at the first motel." He picked up the two hard cases.

Pulling on her jacket she nodded. "Sounds good." She picked up her bag. "Oh." She darted around the counter and picked up the large container on the counter. He gave her a curious look. "Traveling vegetarians back up." She shook the container. "Trail mix."

"Well, we wouldn't want you to starve."

Brent had watched her more than the road for the first hour they'd been driving. "We're at least an hour more from where we're starting, so let me know if you want me to stop anywhere." She just nodded. "Everything okay?"

She looked over at him and then sighed. "Yes. I'm just a little worried." He turned to look at her for a second. "I haven't had any more glimpses and it's bothering me after the blurry one I had."

"Do you think he's been moved further away?"

"I really don't know."

Brent's phone ringing stopped him from saying anything further. "Hello." He glanced at the clock. "About an hour." Brent frowned. "None? What about the property search, did they get anywhere with it?" He sighed. "Okay, we'll see you there."

He clipped the phone back into the holder on the dash. "That was Alec. They didn't get any complete prints from the shack and as near as anyone can figure out the shack belongs to the town now."

Felicity frowned. "How does it belong to the town?"

"No taxes have been paid for years, so it reverts back to the town until taxes are caught up to date. The last owner died years ago." He rolled his shoulders trying to relax. "Alec's going to dig around a bit more. Someone has to know it doesn't have an owner."

"Oh, and chances of finding something there is?"

"Very slim." He grimaced.

The day turned out to be a long, unproductive day. Felicity found out that detective work could be tedious and boring as they took turns going around the town showing Damian's picture. The motel clerk had turned out to be less than cooperative and wasn't in the mood to share information—although they had no description of the adult that had been with the boy, and no date of when they had stayed at the motel. Short of Jac breaking into every room and trying to see if that had been the room, there wasn't much more to do at this point. None of them were willing to let Jacinda do that to herself either.

Felicity flipped through the sketches again, comparing them with the photographs she'd taken at the shack. Sighing she got up, what was she hoping to find a sign that pointed in the last known direction? The motel that she surveyed with bored eyes was only the first stop of four. How long did they plan to stay at this one? It wasn't the worst place she'd stayed, but it felt – well used she supposed would be a polite description and it set off her need for clean and tidy. With her hands on her hips, she surveyed the papers and cups scattered around the room. They'd gotten two rooms, side by side, and she was sharing this one with Jac. She smirked remembering Reid hadn't been altogether pleased with that arrangement, but it wouldn't be polite to toss her in a room with a man she didn't know, so they'd all agreed.

She'd given up an hour ago on listening in on the strategy session taking place next door and had come back to the room to jot down some new story ideas. Her animal friends were going to go on a trip she'd decided. Of course, she'd make their trip more interesting than sitting in a small motel room on a rainy evening. Rubbing her face, she moaned in frustration. If she could just see that Damian was all right, maybe this useless feeling would go away.

There was a light tap on the door before it opened and Brent walked in. He smiled at her. "How are your fuzzy friends making out?"

She almost asked him who, then realized he meant the storybook characters. "They're not in a cooperative mood tonight."

"Animals can be that way."

She nodded. "Yes, even the ones inside my head." She walked over and picked up the papers she'd scattered across the bed during a brainstorm. "Anything new?"

Brent shook his head. "No. We're going to wait until morning and chase the cleaning staff down and see if anyone saw anything."

She stuffed the papers into her laptop case. "And if they didn't?"

"We move on." He leaned back against the door. "They're going to keep moving, so for now, so are we."

She only nodded and then went to the scratched coffee table and picked up the take-out cups. She had to keep busy, do something.

Brent stood leaning against the door and watched her. She flit around the room straightening things. It was obvious searching was causing her as much anxiety as not searching did. "Why do you bother?" He spoke softly.

Felicity stopped with the papers still in her hands and turned to look at him. "Why do I bother straightening up?"

"No. Not the room." He crossed his arms in front of his chest. "Putting yourself through the disappointments. You write it all down and hope somehow it's going to show you the answers." He nodded his head towards the creased notebook on the table. "I've read through that and I'm willing to bet there's more than one of those notebooks and more than one instance described in them where things didn't turn out well and left you hallow."

She looked down at the sketch in her hand. "Not hallow. Quite the opposite really." Her eyes looked at the notebook. "More often than not, I have no way of piecing things together enough to do any good." She sighed. "Not that anyone listens if I try to do something about them."

Brent raised his hands in question. "Then why? Why do you stay within reach of them and let it happen?"

She bit her lip for a few seconds. "I don't *let* anything happen; it just does." She tossed the papers onto the table. "I may escape ones that haunt me, but there's always more – just in a different location." She flipped her long hair back from her face. "I don't get to choose who sends these to me. I don't know why one person can reach out to me and another can't.

So, it's my choice to keep track of what is given to me—on the chance that I may be able to do something with one out of many."

Brent held up his hands in surrender. "I wasn't faulting you for it. I just don't understand how you can stand to do this repeatedly."

Felicity leaned back against the dresser, wishing the room was larger and she could pace around more. "The few times I've made a difference, the very few times, I can't explain the feeling. It's like …" She waved a hand around. "I finally feel as if there's a purpose for it—a reason for my torments. I can't even describe how defeating it is to have this ability and not be able to use it." Pacing over to the window, she looked out at the rain falling. "I often wonder why I'd be given this if I couldn't do anything with it."

He watched her silently for a moment. "Is everyone always a victim?" He couldn't imagine spending his life with victims crying out inside his head.

Crossing her arms over her chest she turned to face him. "No."

"No?"

Shaking her head, she let out a slow breath. "I've had a few that were rare moments of sheer joy in someone else's life. I wished I had more of those actually." She took a deep breath and let it out slowly as she sat on the edge of the worn couch. "I've had some that were the most grieving moments in life. From the loss of someone truly loved." Felicity rubbed her hands over her face trying to ease the feeling of overburden. Looking up at him she whispered in an unsteady tone. "I've been trapped inside ones that were chaos and vile." His eyebrows rose, but he didn't interrupt her. "The article involving a lead to a murder weapon…" She could tell from his expression that he knew the one she referred to. "It was the killer's mind I was inside. I didn't sleep for months after those. I was trapped by emotions of rage and hatred. With the sick glee he felt from killing…" Taking a shaky breath, she looked back up at him. He still hadn't moved. "I'm so scared."

A tear rolled down her face as she looked at him. "I don't know where he is. I don't know if he's okay."

Brent pushed away from the door and went over to her. He sat down beside her and slowly pulled her into his lap, cradling her tight against him. He wasn't going to offer her false promises and say everything would be fine. He'd been a cop too long for that. What he could offer her was something she'd never had though, support.

She shook in his arms as she cried softly. Reaching over he pulled her completely into his arms. Her one arm wrapped around him tightly. Gently he ran his hand down the long length of her soft hair as he tucked her head under his chin. He held her like this until the crying eased, he didn't know how long they stayed like this. When her arm relaxed and fell away, he knew she'd cried herself to sleep. With legs numb from lack of movement, he shifted slowly so he could lay her on the couch. Leaning over her, he looked down at the redness surrounding her eyes and wished he could somehow take the sorrow from her. Moving quietly, he pulled the blanket from the end of the bed and covered her.

Standing back, he looked around the room. The couple next door were probably all cuddled up together by now. He needed a coffee. Walking over to the dresser, he scooped up the room key sitting there and quietly went out the door.

He hadn't planned on being gone this long, but he'd found it more than a challenge to find something that he thought a vegetarian would eat as a late dinner. He'd stood in the all-night café and looked at the menu for at least ten minutes trying to decide on something. *What the hell did the woman eat? Was it always this hard to find something meatless?* He'd decided against anything fried too, she'd mentioned something about tasting grease. Now he understood her trail mix. No wonder she was wafer thin and so tiny, she lived on nuts and seeds. Parking in the same place he'd left earlier, he climbed out and scowled as the rain dripped down the back of his neck. The light was still on in her room, so he balanced the coffee tray and cups and quietly unlocked the door.

Felicity was sitting on the couch, the blanket on the floor now. He started to smile and then stopped. Her eyes were far away again. She was locked in another vision. Swearing under his breath, he set the tray on the dresser and stood there watching her. *How long had she been like this?* Guilt swarmed him and he suddenly wished he hadn't gone out. He moved closer and sat on the edge of the table. The paleness of her skin bothered him and he clenched his fists to stop himself from touching her. She's been so upset not knowing, he didn't dare stop this and leave her in the middle of whatever was going on inside her head.

Felicity blinked and let out a shuddering breath. Moving her eyes she looked down at the floor and then sucked in a breath. Reaching she grabbed Brent's arm and squeezed. "He's sick. Really sick, Brent." She jumped up and paced around the room. "I saw a face, a man…" Spinning around she held her stomach. "We have to find him, there's something wrong."

Brent grabbed her notebook off the table and went over to her. "Write it down. Everything, now before you lose it." He rubbed a hand down her arm. "I'll go get Reid and Jac and then we'll see if we can piece it together."

She nodded several times and turned towards the small narrow desk. Flipping some papers aside she found a pen and sat down. She heard him go out the door but didn't stop to look up.

Felicity was sketching hectically when she heard the door open again. Without seeing who had come in she whispered. "I can draw him, it was blurry. He had a mustache and trimmed goatee and was wearing glasses." Finishing the sketch of the curtained window, she set the pencil down and turned to see all three standing by the door looking at her.

Brent went over and picked up the tray he'd brought in and carried it to her. "Take a few, and then tell us what you saw."

Nodding, she took one of the cups from the tray. "Thank you." She picked up the journal and handed it to him. He took it without a word and went to perch on the end of the couch. Taking a few sips, she closed her eyes and sighed. Without opening her eyes, she started to talk. "He's very sick. His chest hurts, he doesn't want to be awake." Opening her eyes, she looked at Jac, who was standing with her hands clasped in front of her. "I didn't see the man very clearly..."

Reid shook his head. "It's more than we had. In the morning we can ask about a man with the boy." He took the journal Brent handed him. "Did you see anything of where he was?"

Felicity set the cup down and nodded. "He really didn't want to be awake. He kept looking at a window, with curtains." She picked up the rough sketch and took it over to Brent.

He looked at it silently for a few minutes, then turned and looked at the curtains hanging limply with age on the window beside him. "It's definitely still a motel of some sort." He handed the sketch to Jac.

She looked at it for a moment then nodded. "It looks like it." Handing it to Reid, she took the journal from him.

Felicity stood there in the middle of the room. Rubbing her hands down over her face, she sighed. "What if we don't find him in time?"

Brent came over and ran his hands lightly down her arms. "Hey, we know now that they're still using motels." She nodded and took a shaky breath. "I brought you something to eat, which I have to say wasn't easy to find something meat and grease free."

She gave him a startled look and was about to decline when he shook his head.

"You have to eat; you won't do any good if you make yourself sick."

Felicity sighed. Reaching up she gently touched his cheek and smiled. "Thank you."

He smirked. "Eat something, take a hot bath, and try to get some rest. We'll come up with the plan and will be on the road again in the morning." He waited until she nodded then stepped back.

Even after the food and the bath, which had felt great until she'd gotten out; she couldn't stop the panic from rising through her. She'd tried sleeping, to no avail. She's tried working on some drawings for her new book idea. That hadn't worked either. Jac was asleep, which meant watching TV wouldn't be polite. The room was too small to pace around. Sighing, she grabbed her jacket and stepped outside.

The air was cool and damp. The rain had stopped a few hours earlier leaving everything wet and glistening in the clearer night sky. She stood there leaning against the post outside the room. Without turning she knew one of the men had come outside, the silence had been broken by the click of the lock.

"Couldn't sleep?" She heard a sigh before his words.

"Not a bit." Brent went over to stand beside her. "Bath didn't help you settle? My sister swears by them."

She smiled up at him. "It worked great, as long as I was still in the steaming water. But I didn't think falling asleep there would be a good plan."

"No, probably not." Turning, he ran a hand lightly down her hair. "You really should try to get some rest though; it might be a long day tomorrow."

"I know. But I can't shut it off when I close my eyes. I just keep seeing it over and over." She leaned into the arm that still rested behind her.

Leaning down, he placed his hand under her chin, lifting her face up to his. "Maybe we'll have to give you something else to think about for a while." Gently he touched his lips to hers in a questioning touch. When she didn't pull away, he opened his palm and cupped the side of her face, and brushed his lips over hers again. He heard her take a deeper breath and smiled against her mouth.

She turned into him and gripped his jacket lightly in one hand and lifted her face to his. The hand that had been resting lightly on her hair grasped a handful and pulled her into him. Tilting his head, he kissed her harder this time and took his time tasting her, breathing her in.

Pulling back so their mouths were just touching he meant to step away and let her go back inside, but she reached up and placed a hand around his neck and pulled his head back down to hers. Her mouth was open and demanding. When their tongues met in a teasing dance, he had to swallow the moan that threatened to escape.

Reaching behind her he scooped her against his long body and turned to hold her against the wall. Lifting her had fit her tightly against his body, in all the right ways.

Felicity grasped a handful of his hair and held on, not wanting him to move away again. Flames of need coursed through her, and her body reminded her how long it had been since she'd been near a man. Years, long years had need clawing at her.

His mouth tormented her with things she hadn't known she yearned for. Her feet weren't on the ground, so she wrapped one calf around his and held her body tight to his. She'd never felt dizzy from a kiss before, but she found her head spinning and didn't want it to end. When he pulled his mouth away, she heard his breathing was as heavy as her own.

Brent rested his forehead against hers and took a few moments trying to focus. "You took my innocent intentions and incinerated them." He brushed his lips over hers again. "Unless I rent a third room, our only other option right now is my car." He kissed her again, harder this time. "And I think we need a bed, a whole room to continue this."

Her body said the car was just fine at this moment, but her mind was agreeing with him. "Innocent intentions?" She whispered against his mouth.

"You should go inside." He whispered it against her ear. She nodded and then dropped her leg slowly from his. He wasn't sure if he wanted to let her go, but slowly he lowered her and moved a few inches away. "I'll see you in the morning." She nodded and moved to open the door. Fighting his own body, he grabbed her back against him and kissed her hard and thoroughly before dropping his hands and stepping back into his own room.

Felicity closed the door quietly and leaned back against it. Her body hummed a certain warmth she'd long forgotten. Touching her mouth lightly she smiled and then sighed and moved over to her bed to lie down. He'd definitely given her something else to think about.

11

Pulling the door closed, she made her way quickly to the small restaurant at the other end of the motel. Her hair was pulled up to hang loosely around her face, still damp from the shower she'd had earlier. She was still shocked she'd fallen asleep after it. When Jac woke her from the nap to tell her they'd be in the restaurant, she'd gotten up and felt a nervous buzz fly through her that caused her to scramble around and get ready. As she stepped through the door and looked at the three sitting with their heads together, her gaze stopped at Brent. He looked up and grinned at her. Well, at least she understood now that the buzz was from him and not something else.

Brent stood up so she could slip into the booth. "Did you get some rest?"

She shrugged out of her jacket and tucked her bag beside her feet. "A little bit."

Jac gave her a sympathetic look. "I hated to wake you, I'm sure you needed the rest."

Picking up the menu she opened it. "Yes, I was plagued with images all night and was awake more than asleep." She looked up to meet Brent's eyes for a moment and she knew he understood the images that had made her restless most of the night. He smirked at her causing her cheeks to suddenly feel hot. Looking away she looked back down at the menu. "Have you ordered?"

Reid set his cup down and sighed. "We would have if we'd seen anyone to give the order to since we got our coffee."

Jac looked around the almost empty room. "Maybe it was the way you growled at her."

"I didn't growl. I ordered a coffee."

Brent chuckled. "You growled for a coffee."

Reid snarled at him. "You know mornings aren't my thing."

Jac patted his hand. "No, people aren't your thing, Reid." Reid bared his teeth at her playfully then squeezed her hand.

Brent grinned again and looked at the menu. "Is there anything on here you can eat, Felicity?" He read down the list trying to see if there was anything without bacon or ham.

"What do you mean she can eat?" Jac looked at him.

He spotted a cheese omelet. "Felicity is a vegetarian. I found out last night it's not easy to find food." He looked up at Jac for a second then to where her eyes were looking. Turning his head, he saw that Felicity was still holding the menu, but with a grip that had turned her knuckles white. Leaning over he looked at her eyes and saw that blankness there again. "Shit." He whispered it.

"Here comes the waitress," Reid whispered into his menu. Lifting his face and turned towards the waitress almost to the table. "Would we be able to get another coffee Miss?" He wasn't sure if she was a Miss or Mrs., but at this moment he really didn't care.

"Oh, and four orange juices please," Jac added with a big smile.

The woman nodded and turned back towards the counter.

Brent looked up from the position he'd taken of half leaning over Felicity to hide her from anyone else's sight. He looked at Jac, then Reid, and both were watching her intently. "I don't know if she'll come out of this quietly, it will depend on what she saw."

Reid looked over at the waitress and then back at Felicity. "We'll cover it."

Brent nodded and leaned back over to hide Felicity from view again. She took a deep breath and blinked. Dropping the menu, she put her hand over her mouth and looked around quickly. Her eyes flew to his, her hand still covering her mouth. Looking quickly to see where the waitress was, he then pulled her into his chest and hugged her. "Take a few breaths, calm down a bit." She dropped her hand and nodded.

She glanced at the two on the other side of the table and spoke against Brent's shoulder. "There was a doctor." She whispered. She peeked around his shoulder and saw the waitress coming towards them with a tray. "I need to go to the bathroom." She looked up to see the concern in Brent's eyes. "I just need a minute. Order me something." He nodded and let her go. He stood up and turned so she was still blocked from the waitress seeing her. She stopped a few times and took a few trembling steps when she finally spotted the washroom sign.

Brent watched her and was ready to follow her when Jac jumped up. "I'll go, Brent." She smiled at Reid. "Order some food so we can get out of here soon." Reid nodded.

Brent sat back down and looked over at his partner. "If she saw the doctor's face…"

"Yeah." Reid nodded and pulled out his notebook. "We'll track down the cleaning staff while Jac runs a search for all the doctors near here."

Brent was nodding as he turned to see if they were coming back from the bathroom yet. "Is there some sort of database we can tap into that would have photos' for registration or anything?"

Reid frowned. "I'll get Alec to check into that from the station." He pulled out his phone and looked around. "Why don't you go track down that waitress and get the food happening; it's going to be a long day from here." Reid pulled the menu closer and glanced at it. "Just order four of whatever – see if we can get them to take back to the room."

Brent nodded as he stood up.

~

Felicity pushed the plate aside. "I can't possibly eat anymore." She looked over at Brent. "You ordered enough for three of me."

Brent leaned back in the chair and grinned. "As soon as Alec gets back to us, we may be running for the rest of the day. I thought we'd better eat while we could." He nodded towards the sketch pad sitting on the couch beside her. "You get those finished?"

She picked it up and studied it for a moment. "I think so. They had to have moved him sometime in the night; this is not the same dingy room he was in before." She reached over and handed him the sketches of the small parts of the room she'd seen.

Brent looked at it for a moment then grinned. "Looks like they have him somewhere respectable now."

"We're never going to find him if they keep moving him like this."

Brent set the sketches down and got up to stretch. His night hadn't been very restful either; with the taste of her lingering all night. "Actually, the more they move around, they increase the chance of being seen."

"Oh. I hadn't considered that." She got up and started picking up the papers. "I'm going to organize this now; in case we're moving on."

The door flew open, and Reid stuck his head in. "One of the cleaning staff remembers what room they were in." He reached into his pocket and pulled out his keys. "Jac wants to see if she can find anything." He held out the keys. "Felicity, can you get the kettle and thermos out of my car and make some tea to go." He scowled. "She's insisting on hitting the road as soon as she finds anything."

Felicity went over quickly and took the keys. "Go with her." She turned and motioned to Brent. "You too, I'll get everything ready." Brent nodded and flew out after Reid. Felicity went out the door to the car.

Felicity wondered how busy the motel was. Wouldn't there have been too many people through for Jac to find anything? She wrote a short list of things they had to pick up on their way to the next location. A cooler for one, would be a great investment on this journey. Juice and some sort of fresh food would be wonderful. She looked at the clock again; it had only been about six minutes and it felt like it she had been waiting an hour.

With the thermos filled, she capped it and set it beside the bottles of water she'd gotten from Brent's car. Sighing, she began packing up her papers and notebooks. She left the laptop set up, just in case they needed it before they left.

Finishing that, she looked at the clock again. Fifteen minutes had now passed. She hadn't even asked what room they were going to. Walking over she opened the door and stood just outside it. Turning, she saw Brent coming from the back of the building talking on his cell phone. Right behind him was Reid, carrying Jac. Stepping out of the way, she held the door open and waited.

"I could have walked Reid," Jac said quietly as they came through the door. "I'm just a little shaky this time."

Felicity breathed a sigh of relief as Brent came through the door. "Alec found a database for licensed physicians, but they don't have any photos." He closed the door and headed to the laptop. "What was that name again Jac?"

Jacinda leaned back on the couch and took the water Reid offered her. "Rising Sun."

He typed it quickly into the search bar. Straightening he looked over at Felicity. "When we get the location of this place, we'll have to get pictures of any doctors in the area for you to look at."

She nodded and turned towards Jac. "They were going to someplace called the rising sun?" Jac nodded.

"Bingo," Brent said softly. Everyone turned to watch him. "It's a little over two hours from here."

Reid came over and looked. "That would tie in with what the cleaning woman said she'd overheard."

Brent nodded and turned around. He studied Jac for a moment. "You up to a car ride?"

Jac pushed herself to the edge of the couch. "Just a little shaky. I might have a nap part of the way, but I'll be fine."

Felicity set the case for her laptop on the desk. "I packed everything up." She shut the laptop and unplugged it. "Brent, can we stop somewhere along the way to pick up a few things?" She turned to look at him. "I thought maybe a little cooler for juice and things, in case we need them on the road."

Brent finished writing in the notebook and nodded. "Sounds like a good idea." He glanced at the clock. "We'll get the cars loaded and head out now." He ripped a page out of the notebook and handed it to Reid. "This is where we're headed. I'll call Alec and get her to find us a list of all doctors and medical facilities in that area."

Reid stuffed the paper into his pocket and nodded. He turned and looked at Jac. "You, stay while I get this stuff in the car." He went out the door without waiting for an answer.

She smirked. "Yes sir, detective sir."

Felicity laughed and picked up her bags and headed towards the door. "There's tea in the thermos." She whispered. "You should get him to drink some too."

Jacinda chuckled. "I might just do that, maybe he'd stop pouring it down my throat."

12

Felicity wiped down the table again. It wasn't doing any good though. This motel was one level higher on her yuck scale than the last one. Jac had gone with Reid to find some food to bring back, Brent was next door in the men's room grabbing a quick shower. He hadn't been impressed with changing the tire in the rain, and even less impressed with the price the garage charged him to fix it.

Sighing, she gave up on trying to make the room feel cleaner and got her laptop out. At least there was internet here. Bringing up the map, she pulled out the list of doctors Alec had called with while they drove. Alec, she suspected wasn't going to continue being so helpful without answers soon. Glossing over the sketch of Damian was one thing, but when she had taken the phone to write down the names and addresses, she could hear the questions lurking behind the blunt woman on the other end of the phone. She'd been thankful when Brent had taken back the phone to discuss other details with her. Sighing she got up to get the small printer from the table. Brent stuck his head in the door.

"They're not back yet?" He stepped inside.

"Not yet." She noticed the damp uncombed hair and figured he'd been hurrying to get back over here. "Feel better?"

"Cleaner.   Still not happy with the price I had to pay to get one tire fixed."

She grinned. "It probably had something to do with not being a local. Unfortunately, small towns like to stick to their own."

He walked over to look at the screen.   "Have any problems locating the addresses for those doctors?"

"I haven't tried pinpointing their locations yet. I was going to print out a map and go from there." She plugged in the printer and then leaned over to set up the page. "So, how do we go about seeing these doctors?"

Brent stood back and took in the jean-clad bottom a few feet in front of him. "Uh, I figured we'd just go snap a few pictures and you can take a look and see if it's any of them." He stuffed his hands in his pockets to stop himself from doing what his brain was telling him to do and reach out to touch.

When the printer started, she turned around and looked up at him. "Good, I really didn't want to have to go see them in person." She looked towards the window and forgot what she was going to say. "Brent, do those look like the curtains in that one sketch of mine?"

His head snapped around to look. "Where's the sketch?" He stood looking at them as she scrambled to get her bag off the bed and pull out the folder. Flipping through them on the bed, she found it and turned around holding it towards the window. "I think it is."

Brent stepped behind her and looked over her shoulder studying the sketch then looked up to the window again. "It's not the exact same window, but it's the same curtains." He rubbed his jaw. "I wonder if the whole place has matching ones or just some?" He reached over her shoulder and plucked the sketch from her hand. "I'm going to see if any of the cleaning staff is here." He was halfway to the door and then remembered the sketch of the boy. "Hand me the sketch of the child too." She turned and quickly found the photocopy of it and handed it to him. Every time she had that hopeful, anxious look in her eyes, he wanted to hold her and tell her it was going to be all right. "I'll be back. Make sure Reid saves me some food."

She threw up her hands when the door closed. "Please just let us find something that will end this." *Did I get a good enough look at the doctor to recognize him if I saw a photo of him?* She walked over and looked at the list. There were five doctors in this area. How were they going to get pictures she wondered; just walk up and snap the shot? Picking up the page she'd printed she sat down to mark the locations. "Come on, Damian, just give me one solid thing to let me know where you are."

She wasn't hungry. Her nerves were vibrating, and she couldn't find an appetite. Brent finally came back when she'd just decided she was going to go outside and wait for him. She looked up at him, holding her breath.

He sat down; leaning over the takeout bag to see what was left over for him. Looking up at Jac he smiled. "How are you feeling?"

Felicity wanted to grab his face and ask him what he'd found out. "Brent..."

He held up a hand asking her to wait and then turned back to Jac. "I just spent some time with the head housekeeper of this establishment; she was very helpful." He pulled the bag onto his lap and sat back. "Of course, she was more than happy to help me play this clue game with my cousin and let me look at rooms that might resemble the sketch he'd given me to help on our quest game." Reid grinned at him. Brent shrugged. "It was the only plausible reason I could come up with for wanting to know if the whole motel had matching curtains."

Felicity dropped down on the bed in exasperation. "And?"

He unwrapped the burger and took a bite. Chewing he shook his head. Swallowing that bite he looked back at Jac. "There are five rooms with a window like the one in the sketch. Five with the exact type of window from the sketch. I've just come from looking at all of them." He pulled a piece of paper from his pocket and handed it to Reid before taking another bite.

Reid looked down at the paper and the room numbers written on it. Looking up at his partner again he scowled. "Don't even think it."

Felicity sat there and watched the silent exchange take place between the two men. Did Brent want Jac to go to the rooms?

Jac set her drink down and looked at Reid for a minute. Turning she shrugged. "I don't know if I could do five rooms in one day, Brent."

Brent swallowed and took a drink before he answered her. "Could you try two?" He motioned towards the list Reid still clenched in his hand. "She remembered some grouchy man barking at her for trying to clean the room; he'd forgotten to put the do not disturb sign on the door." He sat forward. "With the rooms looking so similar, she couldn't remember which one, but knew it was one of the lower units on the list, and there's only two of them."

Jac sat back and let out a long breath. "I can try, but I might end up unconscious for an entire day afterward." She rubbed her face. "It's a lot to filter through and find the right vibration. If this place is busy a lot of people could have used those rooms since they were here."

Brent took the last bite of the burger and crumpled up the paper as he chewed it. Tossing it into the bag he took another drink and then sat back and ran a hand down his face. "I know." He turned and looked at Felicity. She was sitting silently on the bed with her hands clasped in her lap. Sighing, he got up and pulled the list from Reid's hands. "I'll go ask at the office and see if anyone remembers anything." He waved the sketch of the boy around as he spoke. "We'll go get pictures of those doctors when I get back." He went back out the door.

Jac jumped up and paced over to the bathroom door then turned and looked at Reid. "I have to try." She looked at

Felicity then back to Reid. "If I can find a direction to go and Felicity recognizes the doctor; we'll find him, Reid."

He leaned his head into his hands. "I hate seeing you like that, Jacinda."

"I know. I'm not really fond of being like that either but…"

Felicity knew it wasn't her argument but couldn't sit there and be silent. "It makes it worth it, to do something good with the ability that labels you a freak."

Jac smiled. "Yes." She walked over and looked down at Reid. "I have to try to find that child, Reid. I'd feel better knowing you're going to be there to catch me."

"Fuck!" He said it softly but knew both women heard him. Standing he reached and ran the back of his hand gently down her cheek. "I'll go find Brent and get the keys."

She smiled at him and watched him stride angrily out the door. Turning she raised her eyebrows at Felicity. "If you could just get that little guy to read an address or a phone number, it would really help."

Felicity grinned. "I don't think he can read yet, but I'll keep an eye out for it." She went over and pulled the thermos out of the bag still sitting on the dresser. "Have you ever tried drinking some of this before looking?"

Jac gave her a puzzled look. "No. Do you think it would help?"

Felicity rummaged around in the bag and pulled out the package of tea bags. "Do you get this specially made?"

Jac nodded. "Yeah, Sandy has a friend that's into herbs and things."

Felicity pulled out one of them and sniffed. "Uh! Do you know what's in it?"

Picking up her purse Jac searched through her wallet. "I have a list of herbs and flowers that are in." Finding it, she held it out to her.

Felicity grinned and took it. "You drink some and I'll see if I can find out what these are for."

Jac grimaced. "I'm the researcher, why don't you drink it and I'll research?" Scowling at the thermos she went over and picked it up. "I really, really don't like this stuff."

Felicity paced back and forth by the desk. "Why am I always the one left behind waiting?" She was so used to talking out loud to herself; that it didn't seem out of the ordinary. Twenty minutes had passed since the three others had left with room keys in hand. She'd boiled the small kettle three times now, so it would be hot and ready when they returned. Jac had taken the thermos with her, so she couldn't even make some before they came back. Stomping impatiently to the door she flung it open and squeaked in surprise as Brent was standing on the other side. He shook his head and stepped in; followed by Reid and a walking Jacinda.

Jac looked a bit tired but much better than she had the last time. She gave Felicity and meek smile. "Nothing?"

Shaking her head Jac sat down and set the thermos on the table. "No. I think he was too sick when he was there to pick up anything from him. I thought I had the man's vibrations, but they were scattered and didn't pinpoint anything for me. He was worrying over how sick the boy was and had to come up with a plan, but I don't know what."

Felicity stood there and dropped her face into her hands. *Nothing. How was she ever going to find him?* Two big hands ran down the outsides of her arms. Lifting her chin, she saw Brent smiling sweetly down at her.

"Hey, we're not done yet." He glanced at Reid. "You two want to hang back here for a bit? Felicity and I will go see if we can take some pictures." Reid nodded. Glancing back down at the distressed woman in front of him he grinned. "Get your map and we'll go take a drive."

She took a deep breath to steady her nerves and nodded. "Okay."

At least she hadn't been left sitting in the room alone. Obtaining pictures of the doctors had proved to be a little more interesting than she had first thought it would have been. Felicity didn't know how Brent had gotten the first two; he'd only just gone inside their offices when he'd returned with a picture on his camera. Each time she took the camera from him to preview the image, she'd held her breath. After the first two disappointments, she wasn't sure she wanted to ride along for the other three.

Two hours later, she sat in the car and looked at the fifth picture. It wasn't him either. "Now what?" She turned and looked toward Brent.

He started the car. "I heard that last doctor asking the receptionist to call over to the hospital and get someone on the phone. It was another doctor, but he wasn't on our list." He looked at her for a moment. "Feel like hanging out at the hospital for a little while?"

"Are you going to run up and down the halls and take pictures of anyone in a lab coat?"

"If I need to, but I thought we'd wander around a bit and see if anyone's face rings a bell for you."

She nodded. "Okay, it's worth a shot." She waited until he pulled out onto the street. "How long can we just hang around here and hope to stumble in the right direction?"

He'd been wondering the same thing since Jac hadn't found anything. "I don't know. If we don't find a trace of something today, it's going to be hard to talk the captain into letting us stay."

"That's what I was afraid of." She closed her eyes.

"If you could will that boy to send you something new, that would help."

She gave him a blank stare. "I'm not a two-way. I don't get to send things back."

He grinned. "I know, I was joking." He reached over and squeezed her hand lightly. "We'll find a way." He knew that wasn't as bad as saying "it's going to be fine", but it was pretty damn close and he knew better. He just couldn't sit and watch how distraught she got when nothing new was happening. He shouldn't have kissed her. Ever since that moment, he wasn't thinking with his cop's mind even when he needed to be. He glanced over at those lips that he could still feel and realized half the time he wasn't even thinking.

~

Wandering around the hospital had kept Felicity on edge. Every corner they had turned she had held her breath and hoped she would see the doctor that had leaned over Damian and spoke softly to him. She couldn't hear what he had said; her visions didn't come with sound, but over the years she had become a very apt student of body language.

After walking every hall— they were allowed in— at least twice, they both decided to give up and go back to the motel. Brent had phoned Reid when they got back in the car and his tone had sounded as defeated as she felt. He wasn't squeezing her hand now and offering her hopeful words. He was focused and silent. His jaw kept clenching like it did when in deep thought. He may come across as an easy-going guy, but she knew all the signs that told her he was a very deep-thinking, determined man carefully hidden beneath the happy persuade.

She smiled over at him. "I'm going to go back and soak in the tub until all this tension evaporates in the steam, then I'm sleeping until morning."

"Yeah, I was thinking a solid night's sleep might make the thought process simpler."

She tilted her head and studied him. "I guess you're used to the loss of sleep."

"An occupational hazard I suppose. An annoying one." He smirked. "If we get a call in the middle of the night, they seem to call me first and let me call Reid."

She grinned. "Maybe you don't bark as loud as I suspect he does when woken."

"Nope, I mumble." He rubbed the back of his neck trying to erase some of the tightness. "Do you want to stop and grab something to eat before we get there?"

She thought for a moment then sighed. "No, I'm not even the slightest bit hungry. I think I'm too tired."

"Tired or worn down?"

"You're very perceptive Detective.' She sighed. "I'm walking around hoping for another glimpse— anything to show us a direction." She looked down at her hands in her lap. "It's very frustrating."

"Maybe you're trying too hard." She gave him a puzzled look. "You were all uptight and anxious the other night, then had one after or during that nap on the couch."

"When I was relaxed." She said it quietly, more to herself than him.

"Does it make a difference, what you're doing when you have them?"

She'd never really analyzed that part of it before—always being focused on stopping them, not encouraging them to happen. "I'm not sure. There might be something to what you're saying." She nodded thoughtfully. "I'll definitely try a relaxing bath and get some sleep to see if it helps."

Brent smirked. "Let me know if you need any help – I give great foot massages."

Felicity lifted her eyebrows. "Really?"

"Yeah, I used to give my mom them when I was younger."

"Oh." That wasn't what she had been thinking. She flushed at the direction her mind had gone.

Glancing over at her, he chuckled softly. "I've practiced a lot since then."

"I'm sure you have."

13

Felicity soaked in the bath until the water began to cool. Her mind kept wandering back to what Brent had said about her being relaxed to have visions. She'd never thought to write down what she was doing when the visions hit. Maybe she should start doing that. The last few she could recall fairly easily, but there had been far too many in the past to remember what she had been doing at the time. Drying off slowly she stopped and cocked her head in thought. In her kitchen recently she'd been humming to herself and had been in such a good mood having had a good nap that afternoon. So she was … relaxed. Hmm.

Pulling on her robe she grabbed her brush and untwisted her hair. When was the next one? Pulling the brush through her long hair, she hummed to herself as she thought. They'd been going to go find the location at the lake. She remembered feeling excited; finally, someone was going to do something. Getting up she put the brush away. So she'd been happy? Smirked she shook her head, close enough to happy.

Pursing her lips, she frowned. Where was the next one? Oh yes, after she had cried herself into exhaustion in Brent's arms. There it was again; she'd been completely relaxed in an exhausted sleep… How had Brent figured this out when she'd been trying to her entire life? She smirked at herself in the mirror, *there is a reason he's a detective you silly twit.* He was good at it. A blush climbed up her cheeks when she remembered his kisses. Oh, he was good at more things than his job.

Shaking her head, she turned from the mirror. Focus. Ok, the time after that was … she bit her lip in thought. In the dingy little diner restaurant— laughing and teasing Brent about not sleeping because of him. She'd been happy and happy meant relaxed. Sighing, she sat on the edge of the bed. Brent was right about this. So how could she use this? She'd just have to walk around happy and relaxed all the time.

Rubbing a hand over her cheek, she chuckled. Much easier said than done. She stood up and undid her robe; sleep for now figure this out tomorrow. Pulling the cover back quickly she jumped up when someone knocked on the door. Maybe there was news … She hurried over and opened it.

Brent took in the silk peeking out from the open robe and grinned wide. "Can I come in? I've been kicked out."

She stepped back and closed the door behind him. "Kicked out?"

He grinned. "They wanted some … alone time I guess."

"Oh." She smirked. "I guess I can't make you spend the night in your car."

"I thought about it, but it's cool out tonight."

"I have a couch, or you could use Jac's bed …" She went over to the desk and clicked a light back on. "I thought about our discussion, Brent."

He sat down on the couch and let his eyes slowly wander up her bare legs. "Uh, which one?"

She realized her robe was open and started to close it then realized she wanted him to look. If Jac got to have a night of cuddles and more, she could at least feel appreciated. "The one where you said I received the visions when I was relaxed. You were right." She perched on the edge of the chair and knew it wasn't nice to leave her robe open, but if it was the only thing was going to get then she was taking it.

Brent tried not to let his eyes roam over her, but it wasn't working. Forcing his eyes back to her face he smirked. "Then all you need to do is relax and you'll see more?"

"It would seem that way." She sighed. "Unfortunately trying to relax when I'm so anxious to know he's all right is easier said than done."

"I can see that." His eyes roamed over her. "Bath didn't help?"

"As long as I'm in it, sure—but I have to get out at some point, I can't very well lie in a tub of hot water all the time."

He smirked. "Sorry. Just give me a sec." He closed his eyes and took a deep breath before opening them. "I got lost in that image for a moment."

A warm blush rose in her cheeks. "Oh, I see."

"At least I'm honest." He grinned. "Would a foot massage help you relax?"

"I don't think that would entirely relax me ..." She stopped when he got up slowly and came towards her.

Brent stopped in front of her and held out his hand. He had intended to do what he said, but the moment her hand touched his and he looked down to see her blue eyes darken ever so slightly, his intentions fled. Pulling her gently to her feet he whispered, "I could probably help you relax, Felicity." He lowered his head slowly, not taking his eyes from hers. Brushing his lips over hers, once, then again, he waited. Her mouth responded.

Lifting his head, he placed his hand on her hip lightly and then lowered his mouth again while pulling her backward across the space to the dresser. Leaning back against the dresser he perched on it bringing their faces almost level. Pulling her between his legs, he wrapped one arm around her while still holding her hand and kissed her deeper this time. She opened to his kiss and he swept his tongue inside. Dropping her hand, he palmed the back of her head while he deepened the kiss. Pulling back, he whispered against her lips. "A man could become addicted to your lips."

His words made her knees weak. How long had it been since she'd kissed a man? Too long she decided as she wrapped both arms around his neck and moved her mouth back to his.

Brent pulled her tighter against him and ran his hand down over her tight ass to caress his way down the back of her bare thigh. She moaned quietly into his mouth. He ran his hand back up her thigh, squeezing her warm flesh as he went. When his hand touched the bare skin hidden under the short robe he deepened the kiss. His tongue roughened as he plundered her mouth now. Grasping her waist, he hauled her up against him as he stood up.

He took one step towards the bed on the other side of the room when she wrapped her legs around his waist and moved her mouth to bite at his neck. Shuddering he turned and crushed her with his body against the wall.

Rasping out a breath Brent grasped the back of her thighs and held her pinned between him and the wall. His hardness pushed against his jeans rubbing between her legs. Still, her teeth and lips continued to torture his neck. He pulled her robe up between them and bared her body for him to see. Her pale skin was perfect—perfect for kissing, for licking. Pressing his throbbing flesh into her he lowered his mouth to taste the hard nipple that begged for his lips. When he closed his mouth around the nipple she groaned and pushed into him. Biting gently, she bucked, and he almost lost the tiny scrap of control he had left. Trailing his mouth up to her neck he whispered. "You're so fucking sexy I can't stand it."

When he pulled back slightly Felicity whimpered. He grasped the back of her legs and slid her body further up the wall. Looking into his eyes she could see the hunger he had for her. Pulling up the silk nightshirt she wore, she grasped his shoulder and straightened. He needed no further invitation as his mouth moved to her ribs to explore roughly. She groaned again when his teeth dragged over one sensitive nipple before his mouth closed over it.

The way she was rocking herself against his body was driving him into a fevered pitch. Grasping her tightly he pulled her down to land against the demanding bulge in his pants. His mouth attacked her throat as he rocked against her, he could feel the heat even through his jeans. Turning, he stumbled quickly towards the bed and tumbled them onto it. She was beneath him; touching everywhere her hands could reach. Pulling his shirt from his pants and yanking it up to lick his chest.

The phone in his back pocket rang and they both froze. *No.*

He swallowed and lowered his head to her forehead. In a voice he barely recognized as his own, he gasped out. "If I answer that, chances are this won't get to continue." He held his breath waiting for her to speak.

Her whole body was shaking. *What if it was to do with Damian?* Reaching up she kissed his mouth lightly and reached into his back pocket to get his phone.

Letting out a long breath he took the phone and answered it without moving off of her. "Yeah?" Leaning across her body he let his eyes wander over her. He scowled. "You're lucky I answered. What's up?"

Felicity watched his face as he spoke. His eyes were roaming over her with a possessive look. She was still breathing raggedly trying to bring her body under control.

Sighing Brent reached over and pulled her shirt and robe back into place, then spun until he was sitting on the bed. "Private how?"

Letting out a frustrated breath she sat up slowly and pulled the robe closed. He was back in cop mode now and her interlude was obviously over. She looked at his back and pouted silently to herself. *Damn!*

"Keep looking, I want this guy." He closed the phone and looked down at it. Turning back towards her, he hid his disappointment that she was sitting up and her robe was tied around her. "That was Alec." He snarled. "Reid ignored his phone, so she called me."

"How nice of him." She didn't try to hide the sarcasm she felt. "Has she found out something?"

Reaching over, he smoothed a hand down her hair. "Yeah. There's a private doctor somewhere in this area that came up when she searched deeper. He doesn't have an office or does any shifts at the hospital."

"Does she have an address?"

Brent shook his head. "He appears to move around a lot, so she's having trouble following his trail." Her shoulders dropped. "She'll find him. Alec is … tenacious, to put it mildly."

"I hope so." She noticed his eyes were still glazed and was trying really hard to keep her hands to herself. "So now…"

He gave her a little smile. "She'll be calling back shortly if I know Alec."

"Oh." She pouted. "It's just not … fair."

His eyes searched her face for a moment. Turning more, he reached over and placed a finger under her chin, and tilted her head up so she was looking directly at him. "Just so you're not confused, I'm going to clarify this." He looked at her a moment longer. "I don't want to be interrupted, again. So don't think this is the end of it, far from it. Okay?" She nodded. "Good." He smirked at her. "Now I'm going to go interrupt my partner and he can be as miserable as me." She grinned at him. "Try to get some rest, Felicity." He dropped a quick kiss on her mouth and headed towards the door.

She sat there smiling to herself as he stopped at the door to tuck his shirt back in and run a hand through his hair to ruffle it back into place. Winking at her over his shoulder he went out the door quietly. *Well damn.* Sighing, she got up and then climbed under the blankets.

Brent entered the room and quietly closed the door. He turned to see Felicity curled up on her pillow sleeping. Sighing he walked over and stood beside the bed. He'd called Alec to tell her to let him know in the morning if she found anything, he'd filled Reid in as quickly as he could and then he'd rushed back over here and she was asleep. *Was he the kind of man to just climb in beside her?* He rubbed his jaw as his eyes ran over the golden hair spread out around her on the pillow. She looked like some sort of angel when she slept. Turning towards the couch he shook his head, he couldn't bring himself to wake her up when she looked to be resting comfortably.

He sat down as she turned onto her other side. The blanket had gone with her and now it rested at her waist. He stared at the feminine shape of her lying like that and grit his teeth. *Close your eyes and go to sleep. Don't look.* Not listening, he slumped down into a comfortable slouch and continued to watch the sleeping woman. Sighing he closed his eyes and focused on relaxing his breathing so he could try to at least catch a nap. He could still taste her. The entire room smelled of her.

~

His eyes flew open as a body slammed into him. Grabbing Felicity by the waist, he realized she was straddling him on the couch. He blinked again trying to bring her into focus. She was crying. "What?" He straightened up slightly and tried to hold her still. "Felicity, what's going on?" Not that he minded her squirming all over his body, but he couldn't shake the sleep to understand what was happening.

"They have a baby!" She grabbed the front of his shirt, her face only inches from his. Hiccupping she tried to calm down enough to explain. "I just saw Damian and there's a baby with him now, Brent. It was crying…"

Cupping her face gently between his hands he spoke softly to her. "Felicity, honey you need to calm down. I can't help if I can't understand you." He caressed her cheeks lightly and slid his hands down to her shoulders. "Besides Damian and the baby, did you see anyone else?"

She took two deep breaths and tried to breathe the panic she felt out. "I think … I think he looked at someone coming into the room, maybe a woman …an older woman, she looked kind of hunched…" She closed her eyes and took a few deep breaths and then opened her eyes. "I'm not sure."

Brent nodded again. Even though he spoke softly and didn't tense, he wasn't nearly as calm as she needed to think he was. "Okay, the baby … where was it?" He almost held his breath waiting.

"Uh, in a little bed type thing … maybe a cheap bassinet."

He squeezed her shoulders lightly. "Okay, so it may have just woken up hungry or was wet…"

"Yes." She took a shaky breath. "I didn't think of that."

He hugged her lightly for a moment. Partially to comfort her, some from relief he felt, and mostly because she was on his lap and there. Leaning back, he touched her cheek again. "You get to writing it all down, do some sketches if you can." She pushed up and got off him nodding. "I'm going to roust Reid and get Alec searching for any infants missing in the last few days." Pulling the phone out of his pocket, he paused. "Boy or girl? Did you see?"

"Oh, uh…" She clenched her eyes tight trying to bring the image of the baby back. A white blanket … poor thing crying… bonnet. Her eyes flew open. "A girl, she had on a little pink frilly bonnet." He nodded abruptly and opened his phone as he went out the door.

She was scribbling furiously everything she could remember when Jac flew into the room. She didn't glance up but could sense Jac stopped when she noticed her writing and wouldn't disturb her until she stopped. Finishing as quickly as she could without missing any details, she closed the journal and held it out to Jac, and then opened the sketch pad. "As soon as this is done, I'm taking a drawing class and learning how to draw people!" She hissed it to herself as she started to sketch the silhouetted doorway with the person she had seen standing in it.

Brent stroked a hand lightly down her hair, not wanting to wake her but needing to touch her. When the door opened he put a finger over his mouth to warn Reid and the sleepy-looking Jac to enter quietly. They closed the door without noise. "She paced around all night; I finally talked her into sitting down."

Reid raised an eyebrow. "Across your lap?" He hissed softly with amusement in his voice.

Brent grinned. "Whatever works." He winked at Jac before turning back to his partner. "Anything yet?"

Reid shook his head and perched on the edge of the dresser. "I just called Alec; she'd just received an updated list, so she should be calling back shortly." Brent nodded. "Good." He sent Reid a determined look, which he knew his partner would understand. They had to find these people. Reid sent him back one of his cool looks. "What are you thinking?" He whispered it softly then glanced down again at the woman resting on his chest.

Reid looked down at his phone, daring it to ring. "Jacinda and I discussed an option." He looked over at her for a second then back to Brent. "We're going to take off as soon as Alec gives us a location or locations and see if Jac can see anything to point us somewhere."

Brent nodded. He didn't speak, because he knew how much Reid didn't want to let her do that to herself again, but he also knew these people had to be stopped as much as his partner understood.

The phone vibrated in Reid's hand. Getting up quickly he went into the bathroom and closed the door most of the way before answering it.

Felicity moved in his arms. Brent looked down at her and smiled when sleep-heavy, sexy as hell blue eyes looked up at him. "Morning."

Turning her head she spotted Jac slumped in the chair and straightened out of Brent's arms. Her legs were still across his lap, his hands dropping to rest on them. "How long did I sleep?"

Brent wanted to pull her back into his arms but knew this was not the time. "Maybe an hour."

"Mmm, that would explain why my body doesn't feel rested." She let out a slow breath and blinked her eyes a few times.

Jac chuckled. "I think I've forgotten what sleep feels like. The last few days have been a series of tiny naps here and there."

Reid came back out still holding his phone. "We have two infants in the last two days reported, neither are female."

Felicity swung her legs off of Brent and stood up slowly. "That baby has to be female; no one would put a boy in a pink hat—a girl in a blue one, sure, but not the other way around."

Reid waved his hand around in frustration. "I know, I got that. Alec is checking for a longer time frame— going back a week." He clenched his jaw. "I don't suppose you have a guess as to the age?"

Felicity paced over to the window, then back to the couch. She shook her head. "I don't know, uh … young enough to not be sitting up or trying to."

Brent scowled. He looked at Reid again. "Alec wanting to know more yet?"

Reid glanced at Jac then back to him. "Not yet, but she keeps hesitating before kicking into gear."

Felicity looked at Reid then at Brent. "What do you mean, know more?"

Brent rested his forearms on his knees. "Sooner or later, she's bound to start asking where and how we keep coming up with leads to trace." He let out a slow breath. "I'm actually surprised she hasn't called us on it yet."

"Oh." Felicity looked at Jac, who was giving her the same look that went with how she was feeling. "Would she accept that we're telling the truth?" She looked back at Brent.

Brent shrugged. "I honestly don't know." He stood up and stretched. "Then again, if you'd asked me if Reid would ever— I'd have said no and look at how well he's taking it."

Reid shrugged. "I just prefer not to sit and think about it much, still. The question of my sanity still hasn't been established." He grinned at Jac when she glared at him.

Jac sat up and looked at Brent. "Let's not get ahead of things here. If Alec starts asking, we'll decide that then. Okay?" Everyone nodded. Turning she looked back at Felicity. "Is it the same place as before Felicity?"

Felicity nodded thoughtfully. "I think it is."

Jac stood up and looked down at the floor. "Okay, so they haven't moved again." She spoke without looking at anyone. "Has Alec found anymore on that private doctor?"

"No." Reid said it quietly. Standing up he picked up the phone book. "I need a shower and some food and then I need a computer at a police station."

Brent nodded. "Yeah, maybe we can turn over the right stones then." Brent squinted at the clock. "I'll go grab us some food while you shower and then we'll get Cap to open a door or two for us here."

"Sounds good." Reid dropped a kiss on Jac's head and went out the door.

Brent was tucking in his shirt when Felicity put her hand on his arm. "What should we do?"

He stopped realizing she was more frustrated with all of this than the rest of them. "Talk through what you saw with Jac." He smirked. "If anyone can find something else there, it's going to be her." Brent paused for a moment. "You could also check out other motels and hotels within an hour of here and see if any of those resemble the brighter room in your sketches."

She nodded. "Okay." She patted his arm. "I'll just take a muffin or something light to eat Brent, my stomach is not up to a heavy meal."

He studied her for a moment. The dark circles under tired eyes. "I'll see what I can find." He glanced at Jacinda. "Any requests?"

Jac shook her head. "Anything edible works for me." He nodded and went out the door.

14

While Reid drove back toward the motel, Brent had his head leaning back on the seat with his eyes closed.

Without lifting his head, he mumbled. "This guy is in deep hiding or something. How is it we've got a name, but he apparently doesn't live anywhere?"

Reid shook his head. "I don't know." He let out a long breath. "Other than an expired driver's license, it's like he hasn't ever been anywhere after he got his physician's license." He glanced over to see his partner still sprawled in the small front seat. "The picture on his driver's license is so old, I doubt he even resembles it now."

"Yeah, I know." Brent cracked the window a bit and turned his head. "Let me know when we get back to the motel."

Jac came flying out the door before they could turn the knob. "Shhh." She pushed Reid towards the other room. "Felicity is sleeping."

Brent turned and opened the door to their room. "How long has she been sleeping?"

Jac went in behind them and closed the door. "Just a few minutes. I was afraid to move, she's exhausted." Flopping down on the nearest chair she shook her head. "She exhausted me cleaning and moving things while I was looking up other motels."

Brent stood with his hands on his hips and sighed. "Yeah, she flits around when it starts bugging her."

Reid smirked. "You're getting to know her pretty well…"

"Someone had to keep her company while you two were— busy!" He'd almost growled it and then sighed again when Reid lifted an eyebrow at him. Shaking it off he turned to Jac. "Were the two of you able to dig up any more?"

Jac shrugged. "We found three possible places that could be the ones from her vision, but we're not sure."

Brent squeezed the bridge of his nose. "How far away are they?"

"Two are fairly close together, roughly forty-five minutes from here. The other one is at least an hour and a half in the other direction…" She leaned forward. "Tell me you two found the missing doctor."

Reid shook his head. "No. The only thing we found was an old license photo. It was never renewed."

She leaned back and rubbed her face. "We could try those places that might be the new location, ask around about an infant and older woman … we have Damian's picture."

Reid sighed. "We could be wasting a lot of time doing that."

"Because we're so busy here we don't have the time?" Brent scowled.

Reid looked at him again with a questioning glare. Turning back to Jac he got up and went over to sit down. "Did you grab some lunch?"

Jac nodded. "Yeah, a while ago. Felicity's is still sitting over there untouched; she was too jumpy to sit down and eat. I tri…"

Brent smacked his hand on the dresser and stomped towards the door.

Jac sent Reid a startled look and realized Reid was just as shocked by that as she was.

Brent went into the room without making a sound. Quietly he flipped the lock on the door, so no one would come in and wake her. Reaching into his pocket he pulled out his phone and turned it off.

He stood beside the bed looking down at her. His intentions had been to wake her so she could eat something, but now that he was standing here he couldn't bring himself to. He wasn't sure how long he stood there watching her sleep, but he realized her eyes opened briefly and looked at him.

"Lie down a while with me Brent, I'm not ready to face reality again just yet." She rolled towards the other side of the bed.

As tired as he was and as soft and sleepy as she looked, he didn't hesitate. Kicking his shoes off he climbed onto the bed and curled his body against her back. He wasn't sure if this was what she had intended when she'd said it, but when she wiggled back into his arms he wrapped them around her before she could change her mind. She smelled so good. This felt so good. He listened to her breathing and realized she was drifting back to sleep. He followed her right behind her.

Bolting up he looked down at Felicity; she was looking up at him. "Someone is knocking on the door." She whispered.

Turning, he got up and went to the door. Opening it he was greeted by Reid holding out coffee cups. Brent grinned when he noticed his partner looked like he'd just got up as well. "What are you a mind reader now?" He mumbled.

Reid shook his head. "Not hardly. Jac and I fell asleep for about an hour then woke up and realized you hadn't come back either." He stepped in and glanced at the drowsy woman lying on the bed. "Jac will be here in a minute, she was grabbing a shower."

Felicity stretched slowly. "I feel almost human now."

"Amazing what a nap can do huh?" Reid asked then turned to grin at his partner.

Brent could have cared less if he was there or not. His eyes were drinking in every single movement the woman on the bed made. Reid pushed a cup into his chest and motioned towards the bed with his head.

Taking the cup, Brent walked over and sat on the edge of the bed. He held out the cup to her. She gave him a sleepy sweet smile that made him want to throw his own partner out of the room and lock the door again.

"Thanks." She whispered. Pushing herself up, she leaned back and took the cup. "Did I miss anything important?"

When Brent didn't come back to get his own coffee, Reid took it over to him and then went and sat down.

Brent shook his head and then sipped the magic liquid. "Not much really. The doctor is so far in hiding we can't find anything on him."

Felicity set her cup on the small bedside table and flipped her hair back. "We're at a stalemate then?"

Brent shrugged. "If Alec doesn't come up with something soon, then we're running out of options."

"Oh." She sighed and sat there looking down at the bed.

Brent reached over and rubbed her ankle reassuringly. "We'll come up with something."

Felicity smiled then nodded. "I'm going to go grab a quick wake-up shower and then maybe if we go over my journal entries together we can pick up something."

When the bathroom door closed, Reid looked over at Brent and shook his head. "What are we going to come up with?" He whispered.

Brent heard the water turn on and lifted his arms in exasperation. "I don't know, I'm not awake enough to think."

Reid sat back and sipped his coffee silently for a few moments. "Shit!" He sat in a low voice. "We're going to have to hit the road tomorrow and see if we can hit those places that might be the new location."

Brent nodded. "And then we're out of options…" He stood up. "We'll get Alec to see if this doctor comes up in either of those places."

Reid's jaw dropped. "I can't believe we didn't think of this a few hours ago."

"Sleep deprivation." He stretched carefully so he wouldn't spill his coffee. "I need more sleep before I start driving all over again." Reid just nodded. "Let's try to find a half-decent restaurant somewhere around here and eat some real food tonight."

"I second that." Reid toasted with his coffee cup.

"Second what?" Jac asked from the doorway.

"That was a good idea, Brent." Felicity turned and smiled after she came through the door. A nice meal and some downtime had been what they all needed. She sat on the bed and laughed. "I can't believe you made them make special dishes for me though."

He shrugged. "They weren't special, they were on the menu, I just got them to not add the meat part."

Reid patted his full stomach. "You didn't have to pay for all of us Felicity."

She gave him a stare. "Yes, I did, I wanted to thank all of you for doing this for me…for Damian."

"We haven't done anything yet," Brent said quietly.

Felicity shook her head. "It doesn't matter; I'd never have gotten this far without all of you."

Brent's phone rang and cut off what he'd planned to say. He opened it up and said "Hello." Leaning back against the dresser he shook his head. "Yeah, I left that message hours ago, where were you? You haven't gotten a life on us have you, Alec?" He grinned at Reid. "Why?" He shrugged when Reid gave him a puzzled look. "Uh, ours is 104, but we're in 105 right now." He sent Reid an odd look. "Why would you…"

When someone knocked on the door, both men jumped to their feet and looked at each other. Jac pushed past Reid and shook her head. "Down boys, we're not on full alert here." She swung open the door, her eyebrows shooting up to see Alec standing on the other side.

"Need your room number?" She said with a smirk into her phone.

Brent hung up his phone and grinned. "Alec."

Reid sat back down. "Did you miss us at the station?"

She snorted and stepped into the room. "Hardly. I came to ask some face-to-face stuff."

Brent leaned back against the dresser and tucked his hands into his pockets. "Cap know you chased us down?"

Leaning a shoulder against the wall she shrugged. "I'm on my own time right now; I have to be back in the morning though."

Jac sent Felicity a look. They both knew what the face-to-face questions were going to involve. Going over she sat beside Reid and clasped her hands lightly in her lap.

"So." Alec looked from one detective to the other. "What's up boys?"

"Sky," Brent answered at the same moment Reid said. "Sun."

"Don't make me hurt either of you." She grinned when Felicity's eyebrows shot up. "Relax, a figure of speech."

Brent went over and perched on the end of the bed Felicity was sitting on. He looked over at Reid briefly and then back to Alec. "You'll have to be a little more specific, a lot of things could be up."

Reid nodded. "You couldn't ask us what was up over the phone?"

She walked over and leaned against the dresser Brent had been leaning on. "Not if I wanted to get straight answers."

"Fair enough," Brent said quietly. He turned and looked at Felicity for a moment. Oh yeah, she knew where Alec was going with this and so did Jac if her quiet poised look said anything. "Ask away."

Alec squinted at him for a second. "How are you getting all this information you have me digging up Brent?"

"Various ways."

Reid just sat back; both knew he was better to deal with Alec. He had nothing against the female detective. She was a damn good one. But her ballbuster attitude and his unmovable personality had clashed more than once during the few years they'd been working out of the same station.

Alec studied him for a moment. "Like?" He leaned onto his knees and looked back at her, not giving an inch. "How can you come up with doctor names, different locations and an infant Brent?" She crossed her arms. "Who's feeding you the info? Are they on the inside?"

He shrugged slowly trying to find the words. "You might say we have an eye on the inside."

Alec threw her hands into the air. "Hello. Guys, I'm on your team here. Tell me what the hell is going on."

Brent stood up when he saw Reid had moved to get up. "We know. It's hard to explain—trust me on that."

The tall blonde scowled at him. "I just want to know how. And why? Why I had to go interview parents whose infant is missing and …" She held up a finger at him. "And bring something the baby had been in at the time of the abduction…"

"You brought something?" Both Jac and Felicity echoed at the same moment.

She looked from one to the other then back at Brent slowly with her eyebrows up. She pointed another finger at him. "Don't make me hold a gun to your head. I like you, truly I do but I've been going fucking nuts trying to dig up stuff for you without knowing all the facts and I'm about ready to lose my mind!"

Reid laughed. Then threw his hands up in surrender when both her and Brent turned to glare at him.

Brent spun his head back to look at her. "Don't…" He didn't get any further before Felicity stood up and placed a calming hand on his chest. He looked down at her; she smiled at him sweetly; completely disarming his anger.

"It's okay," Felicity said to him quietly. Turning her head, she looked at the frustrated detective. "I may be able to offer you some answers detective."

Alec crossed her arms and leaned back against the dresser. "I don't care who answers, just so long as someone does."

Nodding, Felicity went over to the small desk and picked up her journal. She flipped through it finding the first one she had, that Damian was in. "These might answer some questions, and possibly create some entirely different ones." She held out the journal to her.

Alec took the book without a word and looked down at it. Without comment, she started reading through it. No one in the room moved while she did this. A few times she lifted her head and looked at every face looking back at her, and then she'd turn a page and read some more.

Felicity went and sat in the worn chair and waited. She smiled inside; for once she wouldn't be alone trying to answer them.

Alec closed the book and crossed her arms still holding it. She looked at the woman that had handed it to her for a long moment. Turning she looked from one man to the other. "This is legit?" Both nodded. "Hang on." Setting the book down, she stared at the floor. Looking back, she shook her head. "That doesn't fill in all the blanks, not even close." She picked up the book and waved it around. "If … and this is a really huge *if*, this is what you say…" She looked at the woman again. "And at this point, I'm not saying it is or isn't, understand?" She inclined her head back in answer. Turning to look back at Brent she shook her head again. "If this is how that doesn't explain why your guys are here, or at the last location … at all." She set the book down and crossed her arms again.

Brent looked at Jac for a moment then sighed. Going over he picked up the sketches Felicity had done and handed them to her. "These are part of your answer; the rest is not my place to explain." Going over to where Felicity had sat down he stood behind the chair and dropped a hand down to rest on her shoulder. He knew she was waiting for the accusations, and if he was in his power he wouldn't let it happen this time.

Alec looked at the last sketch then shrugged. "Okay." She looked at Jac. "So are you physic or something and can just pull the motels and towns out of the air or something?"

Jac smiled. "Or something."

Alec laughed. "Okay guys you've had your fun, now stop messing around." None of them smiled with her. Reid got up from the couch and started to slowly walk toward her smiling. She frowned at him, more than ready to throw him across the room if he came too close.

Reid knew enough not to get too close to Alec McGowan without permission, so he stopped a few feet in front of her. "Could I borrow your ring for a minute, Alec?" She raised her eyebrows at him. "You want answers I need to borrow your ring." He stated it very matter of fact and then stood there with his hand out. Her Eyebrows drew together as she reached down and twisted the old ring off her finger and dropped it into his palm. Turning, he went back over to Jac. "You okay with this?" He asked her quietly. She nodded.

Sitting back, she relaxed and closed her eyes. After taking a few breaths she held out her hand. She felt the warm metal being dropped into her hand. She focused on the vibrations, trying to sort them into images inside her head.

Alec looked around the room. The three others were almost holding their breath. She turned back to watch Jac as she sat there breathing like she was going into some sort of trance or some other weird frigging thing. Jac suddenly sat straight up but didn't open her eyes. Alec stood there on edge waiting as she saw a flushed color creep up to cover Jac's entire face. Her eyes flew open, and her mouth dropped when she looked over at her. "Ten seconds and I'm going to freak right out."

Jac looked around the room at everyone, she knew they were waiting. "Um…" She held up a hand to the others, and then got up quickly. Going over to Alec quickly she held out her hand and opened it for Alec to take her ring back.

Brent glanced at Reid then back. Alec took the ring as Jac leaned close and whispered something into Alec's ear. Alec's eyes went wide, and her entire face flushed.

"Holy shit." Alec said loudly then turned her back quickly to everyone and leaned down on the dresser she'd been standing against. Jac leaned close again.

"I won't tell a soul."

She'd whispered it so quietly Alec had barely heard. "Yeah, thanks for that." She answered her. Spinning around she looked at the men she worked with every day. She took an unsteady breath and then looked at them. They were already giving her an amused but concerned look.

"I just need to splash some water on my face, I'll be right back" Jac walked into the bathroom. She knew Reid had followed her.

He stood in the doorway. "You okay?"

Nodding, she leaned down to splash a bit of water on her face. Straightening she picked up a towel from the little shelf. Without making eye contact with him in the mirror she said quietly. "You never quite know what you're going to see."

"She gets very ill sometimes, depending on what she connects with." She heard Felicity explaining.

Walking back out into the small bedroom area, Jac smiled at Alec. "I'm good now."

Alec only inclined her head. She watched them both sit again then let out a breath. "Okay, you know what? I don't care if these two dance under a full moon and sing bippity-boppity-boo to find the leads." Brent smirked at her. "Just give me the next one and I'm on it. These bastards *have* to be stopped." She crossed her arms and lowered her head to the floor. "I called a guy I know that's been working with a higher-up division on child selling rings, and he's pretty damn interested in this case." When Brent frowned, she held up her hand. "I didn't give him any great details, just enough for him to confirm that they suspected something was stemming from this area …." She motioned around her. "And I mean that like, this area of the globe, not this exact town." She lowered her arm and continued. "Anyways, if we can get enough then they want in and will trail it to the person doing the leading."

Brent puffed out his cheeks and then let out a slow breath. "That's a lot to dig up when we're hanging by threads here, Alec."

She nodded. "I know."

Reid stood up again and ran a hand through his hair. "What do they need?"

"I don't know, but so far you've mentioned a doctor, at least one male and now an older woman—that's pretty freaking organized if you ask me." They both nodded. "Which also means there's got to be enough trails, even very faint ones to dig into."

Jac perched on the edge of the couch. "You said you brought something with you? From the baby?"

"Oh shit, yeah," Alec reached into her coat and pulled out an envelope. "I got lots of pictures—parents always blind the babies with a camera when they're young." She held it out to Felicity. "And if that's the sweetheart you saw, I have the stroller and the blankets she had on her when she was abducted from a parking lot."

Brent frowned at her. "A parking lot? Where the hell were the parents?"

Alec rolled her eyes. "Mom was opening the door and putting the bags in." She made a disgusted noise. "You'd think the baby would be a top priority, right?" Shaking her head, she went over and stood beside Felicity. "She's a complete wreck now. New parents, doing everything right then…"

"I think this is her," Felicity said in a shaky voice. "Her face was so round and perfect." She flipped to the next photo. Then, looked over at Brent. "It's the frilly bonnet."

He came over and looked down at the picture. Without looking away from it he spoke to Alec. "Go get the stuff."

15

Felicity sat on the edge of the chair and watched Brent set up the stroller. She was tempted to ask how he knew how to just pull this and pop it open but realized now was not the time for that discussion.

Alec stood back and studied Jac. "Can you talk when you do this?" Jac gave her a puzzled look. "You know give us a play-by-play kind of thing? "

Jac sipped the horrid tea she had come to hate, but if it helped like the last time maybe it was worth it. "I've never really tried." She smirked. "There's never been anyone to listen before." She glanced at Reid for a long moment then back to Alec. "I'll give it a try, but it takes a lot of focus to not let the heaviness pull me down when I do this..."

"Good enough," Alec said and leaned back against the dresser once more.

Felicity jumped up and grabbed her writing notebook. "I'll try to write down anything you say, and we can sort it out later."

"Thanks," Jac said quietly. "Remember, no one touch me ..." She trailed off and gave Reid a hard look. "Unless you need to." He nodded and backed up one short step. Jac grinned and held her stomach. "I think I'm having a bit of stage fright."

Brent sat on the bed and leaned on his knees. "Anytime you're ready Jac, take your time."

Nodding Jac. Taking a few deep breaths, she stepped to the front of the stroller. "Let's start with baby first." She looked at Alec. "What's her name?" She said it softly and wasn't sure if giving the infant a name would hurt her later.

"Amber."

Jac nodded briefly and looked down at the stroller. "All right Amber, show me who has you, honey."

Felicity took an unsteady breath, trying not to cry from knowing the baby's name. She leaned towards Jac but kept her hand on the paper and her head down listening. Glancing up she watched Jac lean down and lightly run her hands inside the stroller, it was like she was searching for the strongest vibes. She watched her close her eyes and take a slow breath.

"Warm, happy feelings ... contentment," Jac whispered barely loud enough for anyone to hear.

Felicity wrote quickly and went to the next line. Afraid she was going to miss something Jac whispered she stood up and kneeled close to where the stroller was but made sure she was far enough away from Jac that she wouldn't get in her way if she moved.

"Tension ... feels startled..." Jac took a few calming breaths and pushed harder to make her body accept what she was feeling. "there's a man ... no baby, keep your eyes open for me ..."

Felicity tried to ignore the panic in Jac's voice and write. She was holding her breath, waiting for her next words.

"Blonde ... no beard ... he looks so serious ... he's uncovered her ... she doesn't like the cold feeling ..." Jac panted and focused, she was not losing this vibration. Pushing aside the physical symptoms invading her, she squeezed her eyes tightly closed. "Looks like a Ken Barbie..."

Felicity heard Brent get up off the bed, glancing out of the corner of her eye she saw he only stood, making no steps towards Jac.

"It's gone."

Lifting her head, she looked up at Jac quickly. She was standing there taking slow breaths. She was about to get up when Jac whispered to Reid.

"I'm not finished."

Dropping back to her knees she sat there and waited while Jac took slow steps to the handles on the stroller. When she hovered her hands over it and closed her eyes Felicity looked back to the notebook and listened.

Jac lowered her hands and touched the middle of the handle. She inhaled slowly through her nose and then breathed it back out slowly.

"Brent … hmmm Alec …"

Felicity knew it wasn't needed but still wrote it down.

"Inconsolable grief…" Jac slid her hands towards the outside of the handle slowly, trying to work beyond the upset parents.

"Apprehension … annoyance …" She moved her feet apart, so her stance was steadier, just in case she found darker feelings.

Alec and Reid were both standing closer now. Alec had her notebook and pen in hand, ready for the first solid thing she could dig her teeth into.

Jac focused harder, there had to be more. "He's thinking … he's tired of this … this wasn't his part … just had to get to the … hill …"

Felicity wrote quickly, trying to keep up with Jac's sporadic words. The ink started to fade; she shook the pen frantically. Just as she was about to bolt to her bag and find a new one, Brent's hand appeared in front of her face holding a pen. She tossed the other one and took it.

"He's anxious … what's he looking at?" Jac dropped her head forward and clenched her teeth trying to bring it to her. "Red … not truck … he's not happy he had to use his own …" Jac locked her knees when her legs started to feel shaky. "The door opened a woman jumped out and is looking around frantically … older woman fifty … sixty." Jac dropped her head down onto her hands. "It's gone."

Reid was there before she could speak again scooping her up just as her legs started to give out.

"I've got you." He whispered. Nodding over towards the table he looked at Alec as he walked to the couch. "Grab me that black case and thermos."

Alec stuffed the notebook and pen into her back pocket and went over and grabbed them and stepped quickly to the couch. She looked down at Jac as Reid lowered her down gently. Her face was blanched, and sweat was rolling down the side of her face. She was panting and holding her stomach like it hurt like hell. "Wouldn't dancing naked be easier?"

Jac grinned in between pants. "I wish."

Shaking her head Alec stepped away and looked down at Felicity still kneeling on the floor. She walked over and reached a hand down to her; she looked as pale as Jac did. "This clairvoyance stuff is going to freak me right out later when it sinks in."

Felicity reached up and took the offered hand. "I still freak out at times." She stood up and then looked down at the notebook. She read everything and then quickly went over to the couch. Perching on the table she watched Jac for a minute and waited until Reid stopped trying to pour the tea into her mouth. "I know you feel like you've just been poured out of a blender Jac, but give me a description of the woman." Reid scowled at her. She ignored him and continued. "Before you pass out on us."

Jac pushed her hand against her eyes for a minute. "Short build, no glasses ..." She took two slow breaths. "Short, straight dark hair ... she was slightly hunched." Accepting another small sip from the cup of the thermos Reid had hovering in front of her she leaned back and blew out another few breaths. "That's what gave her age away, the hunching."

Felicity wrote and nodded. "Anything to add about the ken Barbie?"

Jac frowned. "What did I say about him?" Her stomach was still swirling, and she hoped she wasn't going to throw up.

"Keep salts near." She whispered knowing Reid probably had them in his other hand.

Felicity leaned a little closer and read from the notebook. "Blonde, no beard, looks serious, and looks like a Ken Barbie."

Jac frowned through the ill waves washing over her. "Yeah, perfect hair. Just exactly like the doll. Not sure if it was real."

Felicity wrote it down and then nodded. "Got it." She looked at Jac for a minute she was getting paler. Leaning over she whispered to Reid. "You may want to take her into the bathroom, I know those feelings she's having right now, and our nice dinner is about to be ruined for her."

Reid looked down to see that Felicity was right. He gently scooped her up and quickly went towards the bathroom, thankful Brent pushed the stroller clear from his path as the woman in his arms started gasping.

Brent went over and sat on the couch where Felicity now sat. He reached over and looked over her shoulder at the notebook. Then motioned to Alec who still stood across the room looking somewhat shell-shocked. "Now we fit the pieces together."

Alec nodded and sat down pulling out her own notebook. "So how many is that now?"

Felicity didn't even have to ask how many what. She sighed. "The guy with the goatee and glasses, the doctor, Barbie Ken, and the older woman…" She let out a breath. "Sounds like the older woman I saw, and it makes me so happy to have someone else see something I saw."

"Four," Alec said bitterly as she wrote in her notebook. "It just pisses me off to no end."

Felicity nodded. "I'm with you there." She looked at Brent. "Any ideas on what she meant when he was thinking "just have to get to the hill"?"

Brent shook his head and frowned. "None." He looked up at Alec. "Where was the parking lot? Any hills nearby?"

Alec scowled. "No. I went there myself and it's level as far as the eye can see. I kept thinking how no one could else see and do something?"

Brent got up and wandered to the other side of the room. "There were none in the last place we were or here either…" He dropped his head and stood there with his hands on his hips thinking. His head popped up and he looked at Felicity. "Those other three possible locations, are any of them in towns with hills … at the base of a mountain?"

She thought about it for a moment. "Not that I recall and Jac and I checked out each one online, looking at the general areas."

Brent swore inside his head. This wasn't getting easier; it was getting more obscure as they went.

"Oh!" Felicity jumped up and ran over to the desk.

Alec jumped up behind her, having been startled half to death. She stood there and gave Brent an exasperated look. They both turned to watch Felicity typing quickly into the browser.

"Oh, which one, which one…" She mumbled in a hushed voice. "There was a sign…" She brought up the first place they planned on stopping in the morning. "No." Clicking to open the next one, she felt Brent move to stand on one side of her and Alec on the other. "There!" She pointed to the screen.

Brent leaned down and squinted at the picture she'd opened. It was one of the motels they were going to check out and the sign in front of it said, "Stop and enjoy the hospitality of the motel on the hill." He grinned. "Son of a bitch, we got them."

Reid came out with Jac cradled in his arms and went over to her bed. "Got what?" He lowered her gently and pulled the blanket to cover her. "She fell asleep after she threw up." He pulled the garbage can closer to the bed then turned and gave the other three an inquisitive look.

Brent pointed to the picture on the laptop. "Stop and enjoy the hospitality of the motel on the hill."

Reid came over quickly and looked at the screen. He gave Brent a vindictive grin. "Where is it?"

Felicity leaned back against the desk. "It was our second stop for tomorrow."

Reid turned quickly and looked at Jac for a moment. "As soon as she's had some rest, we'll make her a bed in the car and go."

Alec glanced down at her watch. "Shit." She looked at the stroller and went over to it. "I'm not going to be able to stick around. I've got court in the morning." She flipped the lock on the stroller and pushed it together before looking at them. "You let me know as soon as you get there—regardless of the time."

Brent nodded. "We'll take a look around and let you know if we have anything for your guy and his team to grab a hold of."

She nodded and then looked over at Jac. "Is she going to be okay?"

Reid sighed. "Yeah, she's been worse." Alec raised an eyebrow at him but didn't say anything.

Nodding to Felicity and Brent she lifted the stroller and went to the door. "I'm just a call away if you find anything or need more help."

"Thanks, Alec," Brent said as he turned and studied the picture on the screen again.

He looked at Felicity, who was reading over the notes again. Turning, he watched Reid sit on the bed beside Jac. "I vote we get as much back in the cars now and try to grab a quick nap while Jac rests."

Felicity set the notebook down. "I'll get everything here packed up." She looked at Reid. "I'll watch her Reid. You go get the car and everything organized."

Reid brushed the hair back from Jacinda's face, then nodded. "Thanks." Getting up he headed towards the door. "Let me know when she's semi-coherent, she'll want to know everything." He quickly went out the door.

Brent turned and walked over to Felicity. He smiled down at her. "We're getting so close I can taste it now."

"I know." She smiled up at him and patted his chest lightly. "Go do your planning and strategizing while I get everything here organized."

He smiled down at her for a second. Lowering his head, he gave her a soft lingering kiss. Straightening he turned towards the door. "Try to stretch out if there's time after you're finished. If I know Reid, he's tossing everything in the trunk right now and will sneak back in here shortly."

"I'll try." Felicity stood and watched him go out the door. She let out a long breath and closed her eyes. *We're closer Damian; you and little Amber hang on a bit longer.* She held her hands against her chest for a minute and just stood like that relaxing the muscles in her neck and shoulders. Opening her eyes, she looked around the room. Maybe she would try to lie down after she got everything packed up. She made a silent note to herself to leave a few things out for Jac so she could freshen up a bit before the hour-and-a-half car ride in the middle of the night.

She shuddered remembering the times she'd woke up alone after more or less passing out, alone. Glancing at the woman sleeping soundly she smiled. Neither of them was alone in this now, and that made up for all those aching moments.

Jac didn't wake up for close to three hours. Brent had managed to sleep for an hour as did Felicity. Reid had stretched out on the bed beside Jac, but Felicity doubted he'd really rested much. Jac was grateful for a quick shower and the food when she was finished. She wasn't as happy about having a hot, fresh thermos of tea shoved into her hand as Reid carried the rest of her things out to the car.

The car ride was long. Wanting to be there quickly made it seem twice as long as it was and Felicity had to bite her tongue several times so she wouldn't ask if they were almost there. Considering she was the one holding the map and navigating so Reid could follow behind them with ease and keep an eye on Jac at the same time, it would have been silly to ask Brent how close they were.

When they stopped the second time so Jac could use the bathroom, Felicity got out to stretch her legs. She'd been on the road so much in her life and traveled more than anyone she'd ever come across. Looking around the small gas station, she grinned, remembering more than her share of stops to similar places while waiting for the next bus. No more, she decided. When they got back home, she was staying. Maybe not in the tiny temporary little place she'd gotten on purpose, so she couldn't get too attached to it, but she was staying in that town. And, she thought with a hopeful hitch in her breath, hopefully with these people still in her life.

Not recalling what time they reached the motel, she was ushered into a room with Jac and both of them were instructed to sleep the last hour or so until dawn. There was nothing that could be done with a part-time clerk watching the office and no other staff here until it was light out. Felicity didn't even bother to change, just fell onto the bed and flipped the far side of the cover over herself. Please let this be over tomorrow was the last thought she had.

16

Felicity sat on the edge of the bed and watched Jac pace. She would be pacing with her if the room had been big enough for the two of them to move around at once. They were, once again waiting. She was so tired of waiting.

"I can't believe what an idiot that guy behind the desk is." She stopped and huffed out a breath. "I've never wanted to smack someone so much in my life."

Felicity nodded. "I can't believe we missed them by a day." She put her hand to her chest. "When he said an older couple with a baby and boy had checked out yesterday, I was ready to run out the door to follow."

Jac sighed. "I know." She scowled. "I don't see what the big deal was to tell us the room they were in. I mean, the vibrations wouldn't even be a day old. I could probably count the freckles on Damian's face with clarity."

Felicity stood up and looked at the door. "I hope the cleaning staff is as cooperative as the last few have been." She walked towards the door. "I'm standing outside; I can't just sit here any longer."

Jac silently followed her to the door and stepped out beside her. They both looked one way, then the other hoping to see the men.

"Why did we get dumped in the room again?"

Jac shrugged. "That was so I could rest. And, if Reid strangled anyone not cooperating I wouldn't pick up the violent feelings."

Felicity looked at her and quirked her eyebrows up. "Maybe I should move away, I'm close to wanting to strangle anyone that doesn't co-operate."

They both turned to watch Brent and Reid striding towards them quickly. They knew something.

Reid stopped right in front of Jac. "We got the key." His eyes roamed her face. "Can you do this again so soon?"

Jac put her hands on her hips and glared at him. "Try to stop me." She turned towards Felicity.

Felicity nodded. "Just go. I'll boil the kettle. Go." She clasped her hands in anticipation and watched Reid turn quickly. She gave Brent and doubtful look. "You should go in case they need you."

He nodded and jogged to catch up.

Felicity stood there for a moment and looked in the direction they had gone. Turning she went back into the room as she silently prayed Jac would see what they needed.

After twenty-five minutes she was ready to go find them. *Once again, you're standing here because you forgot to ask which room they would be in.* She stood in front of the window for five more minutes, watching. Not able to stand still a moment longer, she headed out the door and walked as far as the corner she had seen them go around. She didn't see them. *What could be taking this long?* After having seen how quickly Jac could sense things, she didn't understand what could take this long. She should reheat the kettle again.

Felicity was just turning around when she heard Jac's voice. Holding her breath, she waited for them to come into view. Brent was walking with his hands in his pockets and head down, which meant he was thinking. What had they found out? Jac was frowning, and apparently was feeling okay as Reid wasn't supporting her in any way. She glanced at Reid, he was scowling and had that determined look he sometimes got.

Brent stopped when they reached her, but the other two continued on to the room. "Nothing."

Felicity turned and watched them go into the room. "What do you mean nothing? They had to be here for several days … Damian was so sick."

Brent nodded and started for the door. "I know."

Stepping into the room, Felicity looked at Jac. "There was nothing?"

Jac dropped down onto the couch before answering her. "Little traces, but nothing solid. I don't understand how they could be there that long and not touch anything long enough to leave a vibration."

Felicity sat on the edge of her bed. "Maybe the woman is more cautious, that could be the reason."

Jac shrugged. "Maybe." She sighed. "I picked up little bits from Damian, but nothing I could really grab onto."

Reid went over and looked out the window. "So, now we…"

Brent dropped down beside Jac as his phone rang, he answered it quickly. "Hello?" He nodded and pulled out his notebook. "Okay Alec, what did you get?" He nodded a few times as he wrote then stopped and sat back. "Like what?" He waved a hand a Reid who was looking impatient to know what was going on. "What *are* we allowed to do?" He frowned. "That's it?" Sighing, he rubbed a hand over his face. "No, nothing we can follow yet." He nodded again. "Yes, we will. I'll call you first."

He flipped the phone closed and looked at the notepad. Groaning he flipped it closed and then looked to Reid. "Alec found a private number that we're pretty sure belongs to our doctor." Reid stood up. "She got an address too, not too far from here." Reid nodded and looked like he was going to go out the door. "But…" Reid turned and gave him a glare. "We aren't allowed to do more than gather information and photos… for now. That task force Alec's been talking to is ready to head this way just as soon as we confirm it's the same doctor." Brent looked at Felicity, who looked confused. "We have to watch how we go about this, so no one can get off on a technicality."

Felicity frowned. "You mean they could get away with it."

Brent shrugged as he got up to get the map of the town. "Close enough, if we're not careful how we proceed."

Reid stood there clenching his jaw. "How big is this ring and how long has it been going on?"

Brent pulled out the page he'd been looking for. "From the sounds of it for a few years and it's pretty big to have a task force working around the clock on it that long."

Reid blew out a breath. "Well let's go get the confirmation they need." He went over and dropped a kiss on Jacinda's lips and straightened up. "You ladies see if you can work up some more detailed descriptions of the men and woman and we'll be sitting at the doctor's house trying to get some shots of him."

Jac sighed then nodded. "Okay, let us know what's happening."

Brent winked at Felicity and went out the door just behind Reid.

Felicity watched them go and then turned to look at Jac. "And once again we get to sit here."

"Yeah." Jac got up and wandered to the dresser they were using as a desk this time. "Have you tried looking for some sort of program to sketch things out for you?"

Felicity got up and pulled the chair over to the desk. "They have programs like that?"

Jacinda grinned at her. "They have programs for everything and anything, where have you been?"

Felicity laughed. "Obviously, working too hard." Opening the search window, she paused. "What do I look for?"

Jac sat on the end of the bed and leaned closer. "Uh, let's try drawing."

Both just looked at the screen when over twenty-one million hits came up.

Felicity sighed. "Maybe we should be more specific."

Jac nodded. "Yeah." She watched her for a few minutes narrowing down the search words. "So, when you see others in your visions do you end up retaining part of their emotions afterward?"

Felicity opened a few from the list in new windows to look at them. "Sometimes, the strongest ones are hard to shake."

Jac leaned back on her hands. "Yeah, I get that too." She smiled into the mirror at the other woman. "Do you know how weird this is? To be able to talk to someone about this, I mean I talk to Sandy—but you, you've been there and know like no one else I've ever talked to."

Felicity smiled at Jac in the mirror. "I know. It's wonderful." She looked back down at the pages opened and clicked back to try a few more. "I've decided to stay, maybe find a nicer house and set down some roots." She gave her a hesitant look at the reflection. "I've never thought I'd ever be able to do that … and if it weren't for trying to find Damian, I would probably be so excited no one would be able to contain me right now."

Jac wished she could hug her, and she rarely wished she could touch others. "I'm so glad, maybe you can find one in my neighborhood it's so great there."

Felicity nodded. "Yes, it seemed…" She clicked another link. "Oh, I think this one might be close to what we're looking for."

"Well then, let's download it and see if we can give Barbie guy a face."

Jac lost count of how many unsuccessful attempts they made with the program. "The last one kind of looked like an elf man."

Felicity threw her hands up and giggled. "Obviously when this program boasted anyone could draw anything … it wasn't referring to us." She stood up and waved at the computer. "Your turn." Going over she rummaged through the bag and pulled out her container of trail mix. She went over to the dresser and set it down. Taking a few pieces out she popped them into her mouth and walked over to the window. "How annoyed will they get if we call for an update."

Jac squinted at the screen as she tried to control the mouse to do what she wanted. "Oh, fairly annoyed; at least Reid will." She grimaced at the result on the screen and cleared it to try again. "We'll give them another hour, and then start bugging them."

~

Reid slumped further down into the seat. "Have I mentioned I hate stakeouts? Could any part of our job description be any more useless than this?"

Brent chuckled. "Having been on more than a few with you, I think you've mentioned it … multiple times."

"Have you seen any sort of movement inside?"

Brent scanned all the windows in the front of the house. "Nope." He shrugged. "Maybe he's not up yet, it's still considered early to most."

Reid snorted. "I can't remember the last time I was allowed to sleep until past ten in the morning."

Brent sighed and slid down in the seat to rest his head against the back. "Nope, me either." He scanned the neighborhood again slowly. "Let's hope the girls are having a more interesting time than we are."

Jac sat back and studied the screen. This was the best attempt so far. "Felicity, do you remember which button we clicked to change the shading?" She held the mouse over a few to see what they said. "I don't want to click the wrong thing again and have to start all over…" When she didn't answer she turned to look and see what Felicity was doing. She was sitting on the couch leaning forward. *What was she doing?* Jac watched her for a few more seconds then realized her eyes had the glassy look again. *Oh.* Getting up she went over and leaned down and looked at her face. *It's like she's not even in there.* She bit her lip and looked around the room as if someone was there watching her. *Reid's going to get so mad.*

Quickly she sat beside Felicity and held her hand a few inches over her arm. *What could it hurt, maybe nothing would happen.* Taking a deep breath, she closed her eyes and lowered her hand slowly until it touched Felicity's arm. She sucked in a breath when things flew into her head as if it were a video on fast forward. Clenching her jaw, she focused on slowing things down and picking something out of all the images. Felicity hadn't moved, so it couldn't be affecting her in any way.

~

"I'm starving," Reid said in a flat tone.

Brent looked at his watch and then back to the house. "It's way past lunchtime. I don't think he's even here. We've seen no sign of anyone so far."

Reid straightened up and opened the door. "I'm going to go ring the damn doorbell, and have the camera ready."

Brent gave his head a shake. "And why didn't we try this sooner?"

Reid snorted as he got out of the car. "We were trying to follow instructions." He got out of the car and quickly went across the street. Running up the steps he went to the door and pushed the lit-up button. Glancing over his shoulder to see where the car was positioned, he stepped further to the right so Brent would get a shot of anyone that opened the door. He waited. A few minutes later he pushed it again and listened for movement inside. Nothing. They'd been sitting here watching an empty house all this time. Turning he quickly headed back to the car.

"Plan C." He said as he climbed in.

Brent raised an eyebrow. "Which is?"

Reid started the car. "I have no idea yet."

Felicity opened her eyes and then squeezed them shut tightly. Her head was vibrating with pain. *What happened?* She squinted and tried to turn her head to look around. The movements made her feel dizzy. Moving painstakingly slow she looked the other way and saw Jac hunched over clenching her stomach beside her. "You … touched me …" She had to whisper it because any word made her nerves jump which hurt her head even more.

"Sick." Jac gasped.

Clutching her head Felicity stood up and tried to walk toward the bathroom. She wanted to scream out from the pain shooting through her skull. Her legs weren't going to let her go any further. Leaning over she rested on the dresser and slid a hand down it and felt around for the small garbage can that was at the end of it. Her hand finally touched it. "Hang on," she panted and stumbled back towards the couch. She was so happy this room was horribly small now.

Dropping down at the end of the couch she held out the garbage can. "Here."

Jac lurched for it and dropped onto her side with her face off the edge of the couch over top of the can. Wrapping her arm around her ribs she lowered the can to sit in front of her in case she needed it. "You okay?"

"No," Felicity whispered. "You?"

Jac breathed in slowly. "No." She reached behind her and pulled one of the small cushions around and more or less dropped it beside Felicity. "Lay down."

Felicity dragged the pillow closer and tipped over to lie on the cushion so she was facing the couch and could see Jac. "Just rest for a few." She moaned when another pain shot through her head. "I'll get tea soon."

"Kay." Jac closed her eyes and tried to breathe through nausea pouring over her.

Reid opened the door and then stopped so quickly that Brent walked into his back. "Jacinda?" He went over to the couch. "Felicity?" The blonde woman lying on the floor moved her hand over her eyes and then squinted through her fingers at him.

Felicity was never happier to see someone. She felt Brent kneeling beside her.

"Can I lift you to the bed?" He asked near her ear quietly.

"Please," she gasped.

Brent picked her up slowly and pulled her gently into his chest and then stood and carefully took her over to the bed. She was wincing and squeezing her head. He put her down and placed a hand on her forehead. "What can I get you?"

"Cloth … pills from purse."

He nodded and went into the bathroom to wet a facecloth. Coming back out he looked at Reid as he plugged in the kettle. "What happened?"

Reid shook his hand. "I don't know."

"Vision…" Felicity tried to talk loud enough that they would hear her. "Touched me … during…"

Both men looked at each other then at Jac and finally back to Felicity. "Shit," Brent muttered and grabbed Felicity's purse.

"Have to wake her, Reid." She panted as she clenched her head between her hands. "Saw… a lot …"

Brent placed the cool cloth on her forehead and then opened her purse. He held it as wide as he could until he saw the pill bottle. Reaching in, he pulled it out. "Is there only one kind of medication in your purse honey?" He didn't want to give her the wrong thing.

"Yes."

"Okay, let me grab you some water."

Reid was kneeling beside the couch waving the foul-smelling salts under Jac's nose. "Come on Jacinda, you have to wake up and drink some tea baby." She moaned and her eyelids fluttered.

Opening her eyes, she took a few deep breaths and glanced toward Felicity a few feet away on the bed. "Is Felicity okay?"

Reid nodded. "Brent's taking care of her." He got up and went to the kettle as it boiled. "As soon as my heart slows down, baby, I'm going to be so mad at you."

Jac smiled through the dizziness. "But you love me," she whispered.

He grinned as he made the tea. "I do, and it's a good thing for you I do." He blew on the cup as he carried it over to her. "You've got to stop doing this to yourself; I can't take much more of it."

"Sorry." She tried not to smell the liquid as he held it for her to sip. "I had to see if I could see what Felicity was …" She breathed in slowly. "I had to try."

"I know. I want to find them too."

Brent lowered Felicity back against the pillow and set the glass on the table. "Can I do anything else?"

She closed her eyes. "Give me five." She took slow breaths. "These pills annihilate any pain quickly."

Felicity turned her head slowly and looked at Jac; she was now propped up on the couch sipping her tea. "We better get started on this while I still remember." Jac nodded slowly.

Brent picked up her notebook and brought it over to her. "Do you want me to write for you?"

"No, I think I can manage. Thanks." She let out a slow breath and closed her eyes. Turning her whole body on the bed so she could still support her head she looked at Jacinda again. "I'm not sure what happened for you, even though I didn't realize you touched me—things suddenly became …"

"Brilliant?" Jac whispered. "I've never seen things so bright or clear."

Felicity nodded carefully. "Yes. One moment I'm seeing things, as I usually do … clear enough but not entirely in focus, and then the next it was like I was in the room."

Reid sat on the arm of the couch beside Jacinda. "What did you see?"

Felicity closed her eyes. "Just give me a minute here; it's very hard to focus right now." She went back to the vision; holding the pen ready in case she needed to write quickly. When it started to come back to her, she held the pen and notebook out to Brent without opening her eyes. He took it. "Damian was talking to the baby, they both seemed…"

"Content," Jac said quietly.

"I was focusing on him … I'm not sure…" She looked at Jac for help.

"The older woman came in carrying bags, shopping bags." Jac closed her eyes and concentrated for a minute.

"Damian looked up at the man, the one with the goatee." Felicity's eyes flew open. "He was wearing gloves … uh, like doctors latex gloves…"

"That's why I couldn't pick up anything," Jac said more to herself than anyone.

Reid looked at Brent and waited until he stopped writing. "They know we're following?"

Brent shrugged. "Maybe." He looked back at Felicity. "Keep going, before one of you passes out or forget."

She nodded and took a few deep breaths while staring at the wall. "I could almost make out the name on the bags she carried." Without opening her eyes, she spoke to Jacinda. "Did you see the logo on the bags?"

"Hmm, a white bag … the logo was a burgundy shade. I've seen it before." She clenched her jaw when another muscle spasm rocked through her stomach. "Claries maybe."

"Yes." Felicity smiled. "I love that store, that's what it was." Massaging her temples, she dropped her head and tried to relax the muscles in her more. "She was packing the clothes from the bag into two little cases …" Lifting her head quickly she winced from the sudden movement and looked at Jac. "The children, they were all cleaned up … she was packing."

Jac's eyes widened. "They were getting ready to move again." Sitting up further she looked at Reid. "We have to find them, Reid."

"What did you see of where they were … we need a direction, Jacinda."

"I know." She looked over at Felicity, whose expression was saying what she felt as well; they needed to find more. Closing her eyes, she took a deep breath and let her mind relax so she could remember.

Felicity watched Jac for a moment, then closed her eyes and tried to bring the images back from her memory.

"The walls are really colorful…" Jac said quietly.

Felicity nodded without opening her eyes. "Furniture too, like a theme of some sort … but what?"

Reid glanced at Brent to make sure he was writing. He stopped and glanced up at him. Neither wanted to speak and interrupt the women again.

"Alice in wonderland?" Jac asked hesitantly.

Felicity almost opened her eyes from the excitement. "That's it!" Letting out another slow breath. "What else?" She brought back the images and tried to play through them as she had seen them. "Did you notice the mirror?"

Jac nodded thoughtfully. The mirror was in the middle of a huge playing card frame; ace of clubs. "It's reflecting something outside…"

"Yes," Felicity whispered and sat up; still keeping her eyes closed. "A sign?"

"It's backward… I need a pen."

Reid scrambled quickly to the dresser and grabbed a pen and notebook; flipping it open to a blank page he hurried back to Jacinda. He put the pen into her opened hand and guided it to the notebook he held.

Brent remained still on the bed, trying to see what she was putting on the paper. He didn't want to get up in case Felicity said more to write down.

"Got it … keep going," Reid said quietly.

Jac leaned back again. "It starts to fade now." She opened her eyes and watched Felicity to see if she saw more.

Felicity tried to reach further, but without having seen it the first time there was nothing she could do. She opened her eyes slowly and frowned at Brent. "That was all."

Jac slid down on the couch again. "I feel awful."

Felicity nodded. "I suspect you tapped into the emotions from my visions while you were seeing what I saw."

"Remind me not to do that again." She glanced at Reid, who was studying what she had drawn with her eyes closed. "Can you make out anything?"

He squinted at it for a moment longer. "It's a name written backward." He walked over and held it out to Brent. "The first part is land written backward."

Brent took it and studied it for a moment. "Last letter could be an F … maybe a T …" He squinted then held it out to Felicity. "You're the most artistic one among us, what do you see?"

She took the notebook and studied it for a moment. "Of course." She held it back out to him. "Go hold it to a mirror."

Brent rolled his eyes and then shook his head when he got up. "We're all in need of sleep I think." Walking over to the mirror he held it up and looked at the reflection. "Fantasyland."

Reid was nodding as he leaned over to the laptop. "I'm guessing themed rooms. Get Alec on the phone."

Brent opened his phone and dialed. "Find it and meet the other team there?" Reid nodded as he typed. "Alec. Hang on, we might have something." He shook his head. "No, you seriously don't want to know how—let's just say both of the women are sicker than dogs right now." He leaned down to look at the screen. "A themed hotel … that one." He pointed to the screen for Reid to click. Reaching down he took the mouse.

Reid straightened and glanced over at Jac. She was getting up. Rushing over he helped her balance. "What are you doing?"

"Going to the bathroom then getting in the car. I can sleep, while you drive." She took the arm he offered to help her jelled legs navigate to the bathroom.

Felicity was almost crawling to the dresser when Brent hung up the phone. "Pack it up." She said quietly.

He stepped over quickly and eased her back down to sit on the bed. "You just lie back and rest, I'll get it all in the car." He looked over to Reid leaning against the bathroom door. "I'll pack up the cars and get the ladies in them; you go check out and then call Alec back so we can coordinate this."

Reid nodded then looked at the closed door. "Jacinda, just call out if you need help." He heard a mumbled reply. Sprinting towards the door, he dropped his keys on the desk. "I'll be back in a flash.

Brent started collecting up papers and moving around the room quickly, the bathroom door opened. "Do you need a hand, Jac?" He took two steps to watch her guide herself along the wall then slid down on the bed beside Felicity. "Just stay there, I'll get the thermos filled and then get you settled in the car." He turned to look when he got no reply to see both women sleeping.

17

Brent came out of the Fantasyland office frowning. He leaned down to the window of Reid's car. "Our room was already reserved."

Reid raised an eyebrow. "Alec one step ahead?"

Brent shrugged. "Maybe." He stretched. "Let's get everything in there, I need a shower and I'm sure the ladies will want to rest on a bed that isn't bumping down the road."

Felicity climbed out of Brent's car. "I just need a brief soak in hot water and some sort of sustenance, and I'll be ready to go again." She smiled as Jac slowly emerged from the back seat of Reid's car.

"Considering we've been told to wait until those other people arrive, I wouldn't mind a shower and some food as well." She frowned at Reid. "Are we at least allowed to find the room they were in? They could still be here."

Reid glanced at Brent then back to her. "We're not supposed to, but as soon as you're settled upstairs, I'm going to do some poking around."

Brent grinned. "I'll take the cleaning staff this time; you can try the office staff."

Reid scowled. "Let's hope they're more inclined to co-operate with law enforcement than the last ones." He pulled Jac's case out of the trunk and swung it up on his shoulder as he put an arm around her to help keep her steady. "Let's take the balcony up, so we're not carrying the women through the lobby."

Felicity was grateful for the strong arm around her waist guiding her in a straight line. She glanced at Jac. "Are you going to be able to look again this soon? If we find the room?"

Jac hesitated and looked up at Reid's clenched jaw. "I'm going to drink a gallon of tea and at least try." Reid hissed out a breath. She stopped and placed a hand on his cheek. "We're so close, Reid…" He dropped a kiss on her mouth to stop any more words.

Brent unlocked the door, dropping his arm so Felicity could go in ahead of him. He almost walked into her.

Felicity turned and looked around. "Oh my god. We've been transported to gone with the wind." She stepped out of the way so the others could step in.

Jac stopped and looked around. Long elaborate drapes surrounded the windows. The dark wooden furnishing was gleaming, with no scratched tables like the last few stops.

Brent walked over and opened a door. "This bedroom is larger than the whole last room."

Reid chuckled from the other doorway he'd opened. "Two bedrooms."

Felicity sat down French provincial loveseat and sat back slowly. "At least we'll have more space to pace in." She smirked at Jac; who was still wandering slowly around looking at everything. "I don't know who reserved this for us, but I might have to hug them."

Brent's phone rang as he walked out of the bathroom. Flipping it open he opened another door to discover a closet. "Hello?" He chuckled. "Yeah, Alec we're in our suite." He stopped and frowned. "Oh, okay then." He nodded. "See you in a few hours." Flipping it closed he frowned at Reid. "Alec's on her way, she's meeting the task team here." He waved an arm. "Apparently the government is footing the bill for this now."

Reid's rubbed a hand over his whiskered jaw. "Really?" He glanced at his watch. "How much time do we have to clean up a bit?"

Brent was already heading to the door. "A few hours. I'll go get our bags; you start taking turns in the bathroom." He stopped at the door and winked at Felicity. "Maybe you could find a room service menu and get some real food brought up, just put it on the room bill."

She grinned. "I'd love to."

Jac grabbed her bag up and then Reid's shirt sleeve. "We'll take the first turn and try to speed this up a bit." He grinned down at her, and she blushed. "I want to find the room as soon as we eat."

Felicity went over to the directory and flipped through it looking for a menu. She'd never been involved in something this huge before. Government teams were involved now. She stopped and looked around the room. *How much would we have to tell them?* When Brent came back in, she jumped.

"Hey." He said softly stopping to study her. She looked like she was ready to bolt. Setting the bag down, he went over slowly. Reaching he ran his hands slowly down her arms. "Is everything all right?"

Looking up at him, she hesitated for a moment. "I was just wondering how much we're going to have tell this government team." She watched his eyes for a reaction. "I don't want to be a lab rat."

"No one is going to turn you into a lab rat." He hugged her gently. "By the time they get here, we plan on having enough that they don't ask questions." He glanced around. "Where are they?"

Felicity looked up at him a grinned. "In the shower."

Brent flashed her a big grin. "Are we allowed to share too?"

She rubbed her face against his hard chest. "I don't think I'm up to that at this very moment, I doubt Jac is either."

He kissed the top of her head. "No rush." She relaxed into his arms. "Did you find out about some food?"

She leaned back and shook her head. "I was just looking when you came in." Stepping away from him, she flipped the pages for room service. "How hungry are we?"

He looked over her shoulder. "Well, if we're not paying— starving."

"I could just order up the assortment trays."

"Yeah, oh, and maybe a dessert one." She raised an eyebrow at him. He shrugged. "We need to get as much into Jac as possible, in case we can get in the room."

"Lunch platters it is." She said picking up the phone.

~

Reid walked back in and stopped at the door to grin at Alec. She was picking from the leftover food. "Did you fly here?"

Alec snorted and took a drink. "I was headed this way the second Brent phoned me with the location." Setting the tray down, she brushed her hands down her jeans. "I wanted to get here before the team." She motioned towards the key in his hand. "Whatcha got there, Detective?"

He held the key up and looked at it. "The key for the room of the older couple, they checked out of this morning."

Brent stood up. "We just missed them by a few hours?" Reid nodded. "Shit." He took two steps towards the door, then stopped and looked at Jac. "You got enough left to try one more room?"

Jac sipped the tea again before she spoke. "I think I can do it, guess we'll see."

Alec stood up. "You're going now?" The men nodded. "What about the other team?"

Reid stopped with his hand held out to Jac. "We decided we'd all prefer the team to not know about Jac and Felicity's … skills."

Alec's mouth formed an o. "Yeah, okay got it." She headed towards the door. "Let's go."

Brent turned back to Felicity. "Do you want to come this time?"

Felicity shook her head quickly. "No, I think it's best if Jac and I aren't near to each other during that again." She waved her hand at the door. "Just tell me the room number in case I change my mind."

Reid looked at the key. "206." Opening the door, he waited for Jac to pick up the thermos and then took her hand.

Felicity looked around the room. The kettle was already full and probably still warm, the tea sitting beside it. Sighing she went over to the couch and picked up one of the throw pillows on it. Maybe she'd just take advantage of the quiet for a few minutes and just stretch out. Those pills always made her feel sluggish. Lying down she let out a long breath and closed her eyes. Things were going to get chaotic once that other team of government people arrived, at least she supposed it was going to get that way. She was still worried about having to explain anything to them, but Brent made her feel like he'd prevent any disasters.

She sat up quickly and looked around. *Had she fallen asleep?* She wiped a hand over her face. No, not sleep. Jumping up she bolted for the door and went flying out it. When it slammed behind her, she winced and hoped someone else had a key to get back in; hers was sitting on the table. Stopping for a moment she looked to see which way the room numbers went then bolted in the direction she hoped to find everyone else.

Pausing at the corner to see the numbers, a door behind her opened and she turned to see Brent holding the door open.

"Felicity, what's wrong?"

She hurried over to see Reid coming out carrying Jac. "They're leaving. Now!"

Jac opened her eyes. "Trains."

Felicity nodded. "Yes, a train station." Alec came out behind Reid, already talking on her phone.

Brent let the door swing shut and put his arm around Felicity. His heart had stopped when he opened the door and saw her standing there looking completely distraught. "Jac saw the train station too. Alec's called the task team and they're already finding out where the nearest ones are." She nodded and let him lead her along behind the others.

Alec came flying back still talking on the phone. She held out a hand. Brent put his room key in it.

Felicity looked up at him, and he smirked. "She'll have the locations of the stations before those government guys do."

"Are we going?"

He nodded and tightened his arm around her. "You and Jac can identify everyone involved, so you will be on the scene, whether these other guys like it or not." She only nodded and leaned into him.

By the time they reached the room, Reid already had Jac on the couch and was holding tea for her to drink.

"Is she all right?" Felicity asked softly.

Reid sighed. "Yeah, she's just doing this too much without recouping in between."

"I'll sleep for a week when we catch them," Jac whispered without opening her eyes.

Felicity smiled meekly and turned towards Alec. Sleeping for a week sounded like a wonderful thing.

Alec spun around from the laptop. "Got them." She looked down as the page printed out. "They're going to reach the one station in less than five. The other one is a half hour away."

Reid glanced up from Jac. "Which one do we head to?"

Alec looked at Felicity. "What's your gut say?"

Felicity was startled that she was being asked. "Closest. With two children, it just makes sense."

Alec nodded then turned to Reid. "Can you get Jac down in my car? I'll drive."

Brent reached over and pulled his gun and a spare clip out of the bag sitting under the table. Tucking it into the back of his jeans, he shrugged into his jacket. Winking at Felicity to take the shell-shocked look from his face, he went over to his partner's backpack and pulled out Reid's favored gun. He checked the clip and set the safety and then stuffed it in his pocket. "Felicity and I'll follow you Alec, so try not to leave us miles behind."

Alec stood with her hand on the doorknob and grinned. "I'll try; just don't drive like your granny this time."

Brent snorted and took the thermos Felicity had just put the cap on. Waiting for her to pick up her bag he nodded to Alec. "Lead the way." He lightly gripped Felicity's hand as they walked quickly behind Reid carrying Jac.

Taking a few breaths to try and relax her nerves, Felicity glanced up at the man holding her hand. His face was relaxed; he was perfectly calm right now. This is what he does she told herself silently. This is his world. She smiled when she realized anyone else would have left her and Jac both sitting in the hotel room going stir crazy with worry and wonder. When they reached the car, he opened the door for her. Stretching up she kissed his mouth softly and was rewarded with a smile; his eyes warming as he looked at her. She smiled back and got in.

18

Felicity stood beside the chair Jac was sitting in. Brent, Alec, and Reid were standing talking to three men; who looked completely official. She glanced down at Jac and then whispered. "Talk about anal."

Jac hissed trying not to laugh. "I was thinking the same thing. I'm so glad Reid doesn't do the suit thing every day."

Felicity nodded. "Yeah, those other guys look like they watch too many James Bond movies or something." They both stopped talking when Brent swung around and started walking toward them. Felicity's stomach twisted with knots now.

He stopped and studied Jac for a moment. "Are you up to standing for a bit?"

Jac nodded.

Brent reached out a sleeve-covered arm. "You two ladies are going to stand well out of the way over here and they're going to offload the trains, one at a time." He turned and walked slowly towards a small platformed area. "I want you two to stand up here; if anything appears to get frantic you duck behind this wall area." He looked down at Jac to see if she understood. She nodded. "It will keep you away from all the people and their emotions."

Felicity set her purse behind the little walled area and turned to take the thermos from Jac and set it beside her purse. Reaching out she touched his arm as Jac let go. "Be careful."

He winked. "Always am."

They both watched him walk away. "My stomach is in my throat," Felicity whispered. "What if they're not at this station?"

Jac watched Reid go to the far end of the train on the loading platform. "I don't know, I guess then we'd meet them at the other station"

An announcement came over the system of a track problem; all passengers were asked to get off the train until the situation was corrected. She wondered if this is what the James Bond wannabes had arranged to get the passengers off the train.

Felicity looked to where Brent was standing. He stood there with his hand in one pocket like he was just another person waiting at the station. Alec was in the middle standing beside one of the guys in a suit. Brent nodded over at her when the first people started to file off the train. She knew they were all positioned to watch for her or Jac to let them know if they saw them. Her eyes searched the people as they got off. Twice her heart jolted when an older woman came through the doors. Neither was who she watched for.

A man in a suit came off the first car and nodded at Brent, letting him know that car was empty. He glanced over toward Felicity then inclined his head towards the middle car as people began coming out of it.

A man with a goatee got off, he was holding a little boy's hand. The child had his head turned as the man pulled him through the others lingering near the door. They walked and stood against one of the large, tiled pillars in the center of the boarding area. She still couldn't make out the boy's face and took a step towards the edge of the platform she stood on. Alec caught her eye and shook her head telling her not to make a move towards them. Digging through her pocket Alec began walking towards them; she pulled out her cell phone and began talking on it.

Felicity knew it was just a way to look normal, so she could get closer to them but her heart was still beating loud enough that she could feel it in her pulse. She looked at the boy again who stood looking down at the floor. Turning, she looked back towards the train and searched through the people getting off. Another man in a suit came through the door and nodded over to Brent. Taking a shaky breath, she hugged her arms tightly around her waist. *Where is the woman and the baby?* Brent walked further down towards the last door as people began to get off.

She put her hand up to her throat when a woman came through the door carrying a baby, wrapped in a blanket. She couldn't see the woman's face, but she walked hunched slightly and paused after a few feet to look around, as if she were looking for someone. She started walking towards the man with the boy. Her heart was jumping into her throat now.

"I think that's them," Jac whispered.

Felicity looked at Brent, panicked, they were right there. He held out a hand towards her. Without hesitating, she almost ran to him and clasped his hand.

He leaned down and nuzzled his face into her hair. "Just stroll along with me, okay? We'll get you a closer look."

She looked up at his face and thought she nodded, but everything was moving in slow motion on her.

"You'll be fine. Wrap your arm around my waist like we're a couple." She did as he said. He could feel her arm vibrating and knew she was barely holding herself together.

Felicity kept her face turned into Brent's shoulder as he guided her in the direction of the people. He stopped in front of them and turned her into his arms. She buried her face in his chest and took a calming breath. When he turned her to nuzzle her neck, she peeked out from his shoulder at the little boy. He was looking right at her now. It was Damian. She must have tensed, because Brent's arms suddenly tightened around her, and he spun her to his other arm and strolled them away.

When he got out of hearing distance, he lowered his head. "Was that him?" She just nodded. "Get back over to Jac, walk this way …" He pointed. "Behind them." She nodded again and turned to do as he said then she froze and gripped his arm. He looked up and glanced around, his whole system on alert. "What?"

Felicity forced herself to look up at his face. "The doctor is coming through those glass doors to our left."

He searched, moving his eyes only. "Tall, slightly balding, wearing the green jacket."

"Yes."

Brent nodded once and gave her a little shove in the direction he'd pointed out to her. "Get back over there with Jac, now." Not watching to see if she went, he inclined his head towards the doctor and stood there long enough to see Alec grin and spin to walk in that direction. Unzipping his coat so he could reach his gun he walked back toward the couple with his hand behind his back.

Felicity got back over to Jac and turned to watch. "The doctor is here too," she said quietly. Suddenly more of the suit guys appeared from the doorway and they all headed in the direction of the couple. Felicity held her breath, fearful something would happen to Damian during all of this. She glanced over to see where Alec was with the doctor, she was talking to him in a quiet way, smiling and the doctor was soaking it in without a clue as to what was really happening.

Brent was right beside the couple now and her heart stopped when he stepped right up to them and then smiled down at Damian. He squatted down as she noticed Reid coming up on the other side of them and was almost to the woman holding the baby. He said something and the woman turned toward him. As Reid reached over and plucked the baby from her arms, Brent was picking Damian up and then men in the suits seemed to appear from every angle.

The bystanders from the trains were being ushered to the far end of the station as Brent and Reid began walking towards herself and Jac. She took two hesitant steps and then ran towards Brent. He stopped just in front of her and lowered Damian to the floor.

Squatting down she smiled at him. "Damian, I've come to take you back to your mom." He looked at her for a moment then smiled and fell into her arms. Felicity held him tightly as the tear rolled down her cheeks.

Pulling back Damian looked at her for a moment. His small hand wiped the tears from her cheek and smiled. "Don't cry. I'm found now." He looked up at Reid. "Is the baby girl going home too?"

Felicity nodded and stood up slowly, holding his hand. She reached as Reid set the baby into her arms. "Yes, Damian, baby Amber is going home too." She looked down at the bright blue eyes looking up at her; she was wearing her frilly pink bonnet.

Jac came over slowly and stood a few feet away. She looked down at the boy and smiled, then to the tiny bundle in felicity's arm. Smiling she spoke to Reid without looking away. "I think someone should go rein Alec in before the doctor doesn't survive."

Felicity turned, Alec had the doctor's face pushed up against the wall and was kicking his legs open wider. Her jaw was clenched as she leaned closer and said something into the doctor's ear. The man blanched white.

Reid chuckled and glanced at Jac with a grin before he wandered over towards Alec in a leisurely stride.

One of the men in suits came over and looked down at Felicity. "The parents of both children are on their way here. Would you be willing to take them back to the hotel and wait?" Felicity nodded. "Someone will meet you back there shortly, to get a sketch completed of the other suspect."

Brent leaned down and scooped Damian up into his arms. He nodded to the other man and then turned towards Jac. "You okay to walk to the cars." Jac nodded and put Felicity's purse over her shoulder. Brent winked at Damian. "How about we go get some ice cream while we wait for your mom and dad to come and pick you up?" He received a smile, showing one front tooth missing. Reaching over he put his arm around Felicity as she smiled down at the baby in her arms. He hesitated for a moment and looked down at her as the boy in his arms wrapped his arms around his neck. *This is what he wanted.* The realization startled him. Giving himself a mental shake, he started walking towards the exit behind Jac.

~

As much as they were all exhausted, not one of the four wanted to stay in the hotel that night. They'd answered the same questions for hours by various people from the government suit guys. They'd all taken turns holding the beautiful baby; even Jac did and was so thrilled that she felt nothing of the infant's thoughts or emotions. Felicity wasn't sure who cried more when Damian's parents had arrived, her or his mother. She was turned inside out by the parents thanking her and hugged her over and over again. For her entire life, she'd tried to help those that sought her. This was the one that would make up for all those she hadn't been able to help with. She would never forget this day as long as she lived.

"Felicity, we're here."

Blinking, she turned to look out the window to see her own small house. "Oh. I was off in la-la-land."

Brent laughed. "I think all of us are." He opened the door and popped the trunk. "I for one am sleeping all day tomorrow."

She climbed out with a long sigh. "I'll probably sleep for two. I'm definitely not used to so much action."

He pulled the bag and cases out of the trunk and closed it. "I wished I wasn't most days." Walking to the door, he waited for her to open it. Silently he followed her in and set the cases down on the small island. When she flipped the light on, he saw how tired she really was. "I'll go so you can fall into the tub and bed."

"Oh dear, you have me all figured out."

"Not by a long shot." He leaned down and kissed her mouth lightly. His own body even told him he was too tired for more. "I'll talk to you in a day or so." She nodded and hugged him briefly.

Felicity stood and watched him leave. Locking the door, she sighed and went towards the bathroom then stopped and grinned. She didn't even care about a bath tonight. Turning the other way, she flipped off the light and went straight to her bedroom. Kicking off her shoes, she shrugged out of her jacket and let it slip to the floor. Her life of tension was completely drained out of her, and she planned on sleeping until it was sated.

19

Felicity flipped through the pages in front of her. She smiled to herself. After sleeping an entire day, she'd gotten up and puttered around in a hazy state for a few hours; working out the kinks of not moving for so many hours. She'd been sitting sipping her coffee and reading her email, she hadn't bothered to even read while they were chasing kidnappers around; then the idea came to her and for the last thirty or so hours she'd been working diligently at it. An entire new children's series had just popped into her head, and she'd been working at a frantic pace trying to get caught up with it.

She hadn't realized how much she'd been just settling with the other series she'd been working on for several years now. It had been a long, long time since she'd had any new inspirations. It felt great, so refreshing it energized her. Spinning her chair around, she got up and headed to make tea. Sketches for characters were spread out all over the table and parts of the counter; she'd stayed up drawing until almost dawn before having a short nap and getting back to it again.

While the kettle boiled, she stood there and looked out the window at the grey day. The weather outside might be dull, but the sun was shining inside these walls today she thought. She'd called Jac earlier to see how she was doing. Assuring her that in another day or so she'd be back to one hundred percent, despite Reid complaining in the background. Doing so much had really taken a toll on her, but Reid seemed to be nagging her back to full health.

Unplugging the kettle, she sighed, she'd thought of calling Brent, but had chickened out at the last moment. He knew where she was, so let him come to her. She wasn't a teenager and refused to let her screaming hormones go track the man down—even if he was worth tracking down.

Felicity stopped in midstride and stood there. She could do a series for slightly older children too, oh my goodness the ideas weren't going to let her rest were they? She chuckled and quickly went to grab a notebook and jot down the thoughts flowing out of her mind faster than she could sort them out. When her cell phone rang, she leaned over to see the number. *Speak of the man.* She picked it up without her pen stopping.

"Hello."

"Hey. How are you?"

"I'm good. Slept away a little over a day and then woke up energized."

Brent chuckled. "Yeah, I slept until the bed was no longer comfortable." He paused. "Are you busy right now? I needed to stop by."

She stopped writing for a moment. "Uh, sure."

"If you're busy…"

"No, now is fine. I've been working on some stories, but I can take a bit of a break."

"All right then I'll see you shortly."

Felicity hung up the phone and without taking the time to think about it, she went back to writing out her ideas. She continued writing while sipping away at her tea.

When someone knocked on the door, she smiled he must have been around the corner. "Come on in." She opened a word document on her laptop and started to set the layout up. Something licked the back of her neck. Jumping, she turned around to see Brent standing there holding a tiny black puppy. She looked up at his grinning face and then reached out for the puppy. "Oh, look at you." The puppy wiggled happily in her arms and started to lick her throat.

Brent put his hands in his pocket and stood back watching the delight spread over Felicity's face as the pup tried to climb up to her face. "Do you like her?"

Felicity laughed and the puppy licked her ear. "She's adorable. Where did you get her?"

"My brother-in-law's dog had six puppies a while ago."

"What are you going to call her?"

He shrugged. "That's up to you." Her eyebrows shot up. She pulled the puppy back and looked at it.

"You're giving her to me?" Brent nodded with a grin. "Oh my god!" She jumped up with the squirming pup and threw herself into his arms. The puppy yipped and tried to squirm up to lick at either one of them. "Thank you so much." She looked back down at the puppy, then pulled out of his arms and set her on the floor. Squatting down she held the puppy at arm's length and looked at her. "I think we'll call you Miracle." She looked up at Brent and grinned. "You are so sweet."

Brent grinned. "Let me go get her basket."

She stood there and watched the puppy as it ran around the room, sliding into everything in the way.

Felicity was laughing when Brent came back in. He set the basket beside the island and stood there watching her. He cleared his throat. "So now you have to stay, with a dog and everything, time to settle down."

Felicity got up from where she'd been kneeling. "Oh, yes. Life on the road wouldn't be right for a dog." She walked over and wrapped her arms around his waist again and rested her cheek against his chest. Glancing down she watched Miracle turning in her basket and plopping down with a big yawn. "Aw, she's all tired out already."

"She probably exhausted herself trying to climb up the steering wheel as I was driving. I'm lucky we survived the drive." Running a hand down her hair, he pulled her tightly into his arms again. He moved over a few feet and leaned back against the island. "I've spent a lot of time thinking about you, Felicity."

She looked up at him and searched his face. "Thinking about what?" His eyes were caressing her face.

"Mostly this." He leaned down slowly and claimed her lips. He'd spent the last day thinking about nothing but kissing her. She'd been in his mind when he'd finally woke up and he hadn't been able to do anything but try to find a reason for her stay. Her mouth yielded to his and he moaned and deepened the kiss until they were both gasping. "And this," he whispered against her lips before he lowered his mouth to her neck gently. Her hands went up to his hair and grasped lightly. Closing his eyes, he pulled her tightly against his body, trying to ease the ache that had been constant.

"I think we should explore what you've been thinking about." Her knees were trembling. The words were hardly out of her mouth when he turned them and lifted her onto the countertop. She forgot about the sketches until she heard them flutter to the floor when he began devouring her throat. He pulled her legs open and thrust his hips between them as he grasped hers and pulled her to the edge of the counter. The soft-spoken, easy-going man had her vibrating in seconds. Wrapping her legs around him, she grabbed his shirt and pulled it from his pants so her hands could touch the warm flesh underneath it.

Lifting his head from her throat he ran his hand into her hair and lightly held a handful of it, slowly pulling her head back. Her eyes were heavy with lust. Lowering his mouth, he nipped at her bottom lip and as he reached in his back pocket and tossed his phone on the counter. "No interruptions," he whispered in a ragged voice and then pulled her head back and darted his tongue into her mouth. Her teeth nipped lightly on his tongue, and he growled in response. Taking the back of her thigh he lifted her up against him. Rocking his hips into her, he pulled his head back and looked down at her. She licked her bottom lip and tightened her legs around his waist.

He turned and started walking towards the open bedroom door. She was pushing up his shirt as he went and when her mouth dipped down and her teeth grazed one of his nipples he gasped and leaned back against the wall inside the doorway. When he pressed his hardness into the center of her, she lifted her head and panted out a moan while looking up at him. He let her slide down his body until she stood in front of him. Letting go of her he pulled his shirt off and tossed it on the floor, her hands were undoing his jeans and shoving them down. Before he had a chance to take them off completely, she licked her way down his chest and grasped him in her hand. He jerked his head back against the wall and groaned.

Felicity stood there with trembling legs and looked up at him. His muscled chest was heaving. She smiled when he sucked in a breath as she leaned forward and licked a sensitive nipple. Tasting her way down his body she felt a heat burst into her when he lightly grasped her hair. He was fighting letting her take the lead and she knew it. Licking her lips, she bent down and took the head of him into her hot mouth. His hand dropped from her hair, and he hissed out a breath. Taking more of him into her mouth she felt the muscles in his stomach clench.

Brent's mind was screaming. Her mouth was driving him insane. It felt so good. He felt her teeth lightly graze him and his whole body jerked. If she kept that up, he wouldn't last another minute. Grasping her hair lightly he pulled her to stand in front of him. "My turn." He reached down and pulled her shirt over her head and spent even less time freeing her from the white lace bra that was in his way. Picking her up by the waist her lifted her to meet his lowering head and sucked a hard nipple into his mouth. She wrapped her leg around his, bringing her against his bare body. She was rubbing herself against his hard length, much as a cat would.

Wrapping an arm around her, he moved over to the bed and lowered her to it as he moved his mouth over to tease the other nipple. Her hands were weaved into his hair and holding his head against her. Pulling back, he stood up and looked down at her with her hair fanned out around her. Kneeling on one knee he reached down and ran a hand lightly from her collar bone to the top of her jeans. Flicking the button open, he ran the back of his fingers lightly under the material. Her breathing was as ragged as his own. "I'd like to say I was going to go slow, but I don't think I can right now."

"Just don't stop." Her voice was so husky she barely recognized it.

He grinned at her as he unzipped the jeans and pulled them over her hips. "I won't." When he pulled the jeans off her legs he stood there and looked down at her. Grasping himself tightly he slid his hand up and down a few times. "You are so fucking sexy, Felicity." Leaning over he kneeled on the bed again and slid a hand under her and lifted the weight of her upper body until she was sitting. In one movement he was kneeling between her legs with her straddling his thighs. She wrapped her arms around his neck and bit his neck. "Wrap your legs around me. Now." He kissed her hard as he lifted her up over him. When her legs touched his side, he plunged up into her in one movement. She cried out and dropped her head back.

Hissing out a breath, he fought for control. "You're so tight." Pulling her mouth back to his he kissed her roughly as he moved her body up and down him. She whimpered against his lips each time their bodies connected. Her hands gripped his shoulders tightly as she started rocking against his body every time he lowered her. Leaning his head back he grasped her waist with both hands and increased the speed. She looked like a dream with her long hair surrounding her as she threw her head back and gasped with each stroke he made.

What was left of his control broke when she started to moan louder. He thrust her down onto him as his hips rocked up into her, harder and faster with each stroke. She cried out and he felt the heat flow over him as she shuddered. Gritting his teeth, he frantically thrust up into her while slamming her down onto him. He held his breath when his release rocked through him while she was still convulsing around him.

Felicity dropped her head forward onto his shoulder and tried to catch her breath. She actually felt dizzy and lightheaded from climaxing so quickly. Kissing the side of his neck she grinned when he shuddered against her.

Dropping his head down, he kissed her shoulder. Balancing her weight between her shoulder blades he lowered them both to the bed; not wanting to pull out just yet. She relaxed under him and began kissing his neck and shoulders. His arms weren't as steady as he'd like, so he flipped them in one swift movement so she lay on his chest. Her mouth was still moving over his skin, tasting him. "You keep doing that and I won't even get a chance to catch my breath." She lifted her head and smiled down at him. Reaching he held her face lightly in his hands and lifted his mouth to hers.

His kiss was so gentle and thorough that she sighed when he stopped and smiled at her. "So, you like the puppy?"

She laughed softly. "I like the guy that gave me the puppy too."

"I'm glad to hear that because I think he wants to spend a lot more time with you."

She sat up on him, sighing when she felt him getting hard inside her. "He does?"

"Yeah, he does—a lot." He grasped her waist lightly and lifted her to slide up him slowly.

"I'm happy to hear that." When he lowered her back down, she moaned quietly.

He lifted her again slowly and felt her clench around him. Lifting his head to taste her he stopped when she suddenly went stiff. He looked up at her to see her laughing and looking beside the bed. Turning his head, he looked to see Miracle sitting beside it wagging her tail. He groaned. "You made me

forget to close the door." He ran a hand over her bottom. "I was just getting started."
She laughed at him. "I didn't make you do anything detective." She leaned down and kissed him roughly. "And you'll just have to start all over later now." Lifting off of him she scooted to the edge of the bed. Reaching down she rubbed the puppy's tummy as it dropped onto its back. She looked over at the man watching her with adoration in his eyes and couldn't remember ever being happier than she was right at this moment.

The Witch Within

Ancestor's Enchantment Trilogy

Book 1

By Jacqueline Paige

Prologue

The sun was long past setting as the six gathered deep in the darkness and began moving through the trees. Their only light was that of the luminescent moon at its fullest. The youngest of the six led the way, she may have been the least in years, yet the others knew she was the one that held all the strength.

In her wake, each would turn and check their trail to be certain no one followed. If their parents were ever to know, it would be the end of them all. The power and gifts they held secret had been discovered quite by accident a few years before, since that time they had honed their great skills of true magic.

Eden quickly caught up to her sister at the front, a sister of choice and not from blood. Ducking her head, she whispered as close to Alana's ear as she possibly could. "Do you know of the reason for the summoning?"

Alana shook her pitch-black hair back from her face. "I do not." She turned towards the lake and increased the pace of her step. Peering back over her shoulder, she gauged the others closeness and then spoke as soft as a breeze. "A dark feeling has filled me for many days past, I fear it is not for good reasons we gather on this autumnal night." She patted the bundle she carried from a cord at her side. "We must be wary and prepared."

Eden inhaled sharply and dropped back a pace. "I shall caution Bridget."

Alana only lifted her face to the moon's rays and continued on. Turning to look quickly at the three that walked a ways behind, heads close together, she turned and gave Bridget a stare to bring her to hasten her movement forward. As soon as she was within hearing, she whispered to the ground. "Alana has dark feelings-yet again."

Bridget sighed quite loudly. "I have been a feared of such since two days' past, she walks about with that crease on her brow and my guts supposed it was to be brusquely that our scheme was at hand."

Eden nodded, but daren't say more for fear of the others overhearing.

Once reaching the lake, the six spread out the distance between their bodies, in habit, a circle was formed. Alana set her bundle upon the ground at her feet and turned to the eldest among them. "Having done as you stated, not one of us has uttered a query for this assembly you have called, Ella." She looked around at her sisters of her choosing to see their rapt attention on the one she spoke to. "Do end our curiosity, sister, and share the meaning, if you please." She kept her focus on the crimson-haired sister, watching for a sign she prayed would not be revealed. Ella flipped her long locks back as she let her eyes move over each girl present. The last she looked upon was Alana, as she knew to be common with her.

"It is my right to call each of you—as only sisters of our circle apt to do." Lenora and Jane were the only of the five that agreed readily. "The year is now one thousand, six hundred eighty-five. It has been five years past, since the night we found our way to one another, as we are. I have a wish to

ensure the threats to our very lives are secure and to behold a power that we six are deserving of."

Alana shook her head when Eden inhaled raggedly. "Sister, Ella, have we not spoke of this to the point of tiring? The hunts have ceased, no more shall be accused nor sought. We are here, each one of us safe." She glanced at the others and found the group was as she knew it to be, split into two groups of three. "Not once during the trials and fearsome times did even one come to think of us as a sort of betrayer to the word..."

"Alana, child, you are what now? Ten and three years?" Ella smiled in that maddening way she had. "I, having five further years on yours can feel it in my bones, these outrageous happenings are not at a cease and we are very much in need of ensuring it does not come to pass again."

Alana dropped her head down and let her black hair cover her face whilst she sought out the vibrations of the others dear to her heart. Lifting her face, she beheld the moon hanging over the lake. "We are but children, Ella. As god-fearing as any that step in the arch of our church, we have nothing to fear."

"We have everything to fear!" Ella's voice rose through the silence of the night. "I shall be a betrothed woman in a short time and then what will become of me when my husband discovers what I am?"

Eden replied before Alana had the chance. "I am certain William will be ignorant of your habits, sister. How would he ever find a clue unless you told him you are a witch of magicks."

Lenora stepped forward and shook her head. "In less than the years we have been together, each of us shall be wives—then what shall we ever do?"

"I agree," Jane said quietly. "In one year's time, I too will be set to marry."

Bridget lifted her head and glared at Jane. "Whoever shall marry you shall get what he has coming to him."

Tiring from the words they had all said to her many times before, Alana raised her hands in the air and sent a gust of wind through the circle. "I cannot bear to hear this again, sisters." She turned and watched as Ella and Jane nodded to one another. "I am not taking part in your scheme of evil darkness."

Ella snorted in an unpleasant manner. "You would break your word to each present here?"

Alana took a step back, bringing her close to the water's edge. "I would not." Her eyes quickly met that of Eden and Bridget before she finished. "I would choose to revoke all that I have been given than do unjust things to others that cannot defend themselves from your dark ways."

Lenora gasped. "You would not..."

Alana raised her hands. "I would exactly."

Jane stepped in front of Ella. "For you to revoke your gifts, would you not be obliged to take all of ours?"

Alana shrugged. "Mayhap it will take all, no one can be certain."

Ella shoved Jane out of her way. "You would not dare to try, young sister..."

Eden bent down at Alana's feet and opened the bundle. Alana opened her hands in front of her and bit her lip to stop from hissing as her sister placed a small score on each of her palms. Keeping her focus on the three opposed, she prayed they could not see. When Eden straightened and walked past Bridget, she knew the task was complete.

Alana clasped a hand each of Eden and Bridget and raised their arms; the blood from the shallow scores upon their hands mixed and brought to her a heat of power that only she could have born.

"Sister, Eden, stop them!" Lenora cried.

Alana closed her eyes and felt the winds circle her with recognition. Beneath her feet the ground quivered, waiting for her to speak to it. As she opened her eyes and focused on the three sisters she did not now touch, she felt the spray from the water at her back cover her in small droplets. "I cannot be part of something that goes against all that I feel to be right, sisters." Tilting her head, she looked at Jane. "Join us in protecting what is just."

Jane's eyes widened and for the briefness of a heartbeat, Alana thought there was a small chance she might agree, but she shook her head and stepped beside Ella. Woefulness filled her insides, and even though she knew the outcome days before, her heart begged her to attempt. "Lenora?" Once more she waited even though she knew another sister was lost to her. Lenora backed further away and looked at the sand under her feet. "So shall it be," Alana whispered.

Inhaling slowly, she raised her eyes to the moon whose rays bound her to the sky above. "I call ..."

"Wait!" Ella's voice was filled with panic. "We can speak more of this and draw an end that pleases each one of us together."

The fear jolted into her from the hands she held. Without looking at Ella, she sought to feel what was in her soul. Pain enveloped her heart as the truth coursed into her. "Why speak of falseness, eldest sister? I know what lurks in your heart and I must protect the innocent you wish to cause sufferance to."

Raising her hands higher she spoke to the night. "I call upon the night and all of her energy, come to me and abet me with this, my last task." The winds swirled colored leaves around her, she smiled and let the magic wash over, feeling the warm welcome of it just once more. Lightning streaked through the clear sky above, she inhaled the power. "I seek to bind this three and three from doing any harm." A circle of flames burst around them, flicking as long tongues of three feet high, blocking the outside from entering and the six from leaving. "I send for safe keeping all that we have, the gifts that you gave, to our furthest ancestors to keep within until there is a dire need of them."

A stinging traveled along her flesh as the energies gathered, waiting for her leave go of. "When a time comes that this three and three be together once more, awaken and come again..." So much power was collecting inside her that she had no choice but to cry a single tear, knowing that this was the last time she would feel it in this body. "Collect inside the generations and carry us forward to a time long from now." She could hear crying but was not to take a chance to see which sister or sisters it came from. "Select the one that bears goodwill, hold an honest heart, and make her remember. Remember the times of this six and behold the gifts we pass to her." A clap of thunder sounded across the sky, its cry echoing over the lake until it faded back into the night. "I thank you from deep within and now set you free..."

A strong tunnel of wind gusted through the circle, stealing any more she had to speak. Opening her eyes wider she watched as each sister dropped to the ground, leaving her the last one standing. A burning washed over her, pulling at her until she thought she could bear it no longer, and then it was gone. Emptiness filled her as the flames swallowed into the ground. Behind her, the water was now lying calmly as it had been when they had arrived. The earth was now silent, as it had been. The rays of the moon seemed no more than a light in the darkness, without power and purpose.

A draining feeling passed through her, causing her legs to weaken under her until she dropped onto the sand and panted to seek to breathe once again. Looking around, the others didn't move, they just lay where they had fallen without a word. When she glanced upon Ella, the hatred was clearly on her face.

"I will have vengeance." Ella hissed at her.

Alana rolled onto her back and looked at the sky, feeling like nothing more than a child again. "You may seek to strive for such." She answered softly. "My will shall fall to my kin far from now and we shall see if you find triumph." To feel nothing but commonness once more—it was wondrous to feel.

1

Was she floating? See seemed weightless enough to be. Squeezing her eyes shut, she counted to ten before opening them again.

Hovering above a lake, she could see her own shadow cast on the water from the moon above her.

A dream, it had to be a dream. The last time she checked none of her life skills involved floating.

Glancing around, she didn't recognize the area below her. People were walking through trees, or maybe those were just children...

Where was she?

A void feeling came over her like she was fading...

What was that ringing noise?

Bolting up, Teegan looked around to realize she was in her own living room.

Dropping her head down, she heaved out a loud breath. *The dreams were just getting weirder and weirder.* She froze—why was she sleeping on her couch? She remembered climbing into bed the night before, didn't she? Her pills were the only solution her groggy mind gave her. She must have forgotten to take one sometime yesterday. It had happened before, one day blurred with another and she lost track.

Sighing, she reached for the bottle of water. It fell to the floor. Either she was still half asleep or she had just managed to knock a bottle to the floor without even touching it. It was going to be one of those days...

The phone ringing jolted her back to reality. Scrambling across the room, she grabbed it.

"Took you long enough to answer. Come on, we're going to be late!"

Turning to the clock she gasped. "Cripes! Give me five minutes, Kat." Hanging up the phone she spun around trying to decide what she needed. "I can't believe this is happening again!" Running into the bathroom, she quickly brushed her teeth and hair.

Surveying her reflection in the mirror, she stopped and held her breath. When exactly had she put on her long sundress? Turning, she peeked into the bedroom to see the clothes she had taken off the night before sitting on the chair. On the floor beside the bed were the pj's. *What was going on? Was she blacking out now as well as having messed up dreams?* Shaking her head, she spun back to the mirror and made the call that the dress stayed, she didn't have time to find something else to wear. *What day was it?* Please don't be Wednesday, she couldn't handle a meeting today. Tossing the brush onto the counter, she grabbed her makeup bag and the bottle of pills and shook them as she bolted out of the room. "Why aren't you working?"

Black shoes or white? Hitting the hallway at a jog, she grabbed folders off the table and stuffed them into her bag along with her cell phone. *Keys, where are they this time?* Shoving a foot into her black pumps as she looked around the room for the ever-elusive keys, spotting them, on the counter, she quickly put on the other shoe and darted over to get them.

Tossing her bag over the seat, she climbed in and slammed the door.

"Four minutes and fifty-two seconds. That's a record for you, Teeg."

Huffing out a breath she turned to look at Kat. "I slept in." Kat made a strangled noise that could have been a snort, possibly a laugh.

"I gathered." With her usual heavy foot, Kat shot the car into traffic.

Teegan dug through her make-up bag and then flipped down the mirror. "Cripes, I look like a corpse."

"I'd ask if you had one of your wild dreams again, but I think I know the answer."

"This is the fourth one in the last two weeks. I don't think the doctor's wonderful pills are doing their job." She attempted to cover the dark circles under her eyes. "I took one at lunch yesterday, didn't I?"

Kat swerved the car around a cyclist. "They need their own damn lane. Uh, yeah, I'm pretty sure you did take one. Why?"

Checking their path to make sure there were no obstacles before she raised the mascara to her eye, Teegan sighed. "I wasn't sure if I did. I must not be taking them regularly enough lately or something…"

"Or the doctor's a quack, I've been telling you that all along."

Teegan dropped her makeup bag into the back seat. "Will I pass as alive?"

A quick glance from Kat made her smile. "You look sexy and exotic no matter what you do. I really hate that you have six miles of perfectly straight undyed black hair you know."

"Your hair is lovely."

Kat snorted, "My hair is mud-colored fuzz and we both know it."

Shaking her head, Teegan leaned back against the seat, it was safer to be braced for anything with her crazy friends driving. "You fit into the cute category and that is a far better thing."

"Whatever…" Her cell phone buzzed from the dashboard. Grinning, Kat hit speaker. "Hey, Ann. Are you there yet?"

"Early as planned."

Teegan sat up straight. "New girl there yet?"

"Yep."

Kat smacked her hands off the steering wheel. "And?"

"I don't like her."

"You don't like anyone." Rolling her eyes at Kat, she smirked.

"Wrong, well, okay possibly true. She's snotty and I get bad vibes crawling all over my skin when I look at her."

Kat tapped her fingers on the wheel as she waited for the light to change. "Last time you had your bad vibes, I ended up having to work for that mutant Ernest." She accelerated through the light before most other drivers had a chance to even realize it was green.

"We'll be there in five minutes, Ann. I'm going to hang up before Kat gets us killed." Reaching over she hung up the phone.

"Hey. I wanted more intel."

Teegan smiled at her. "We'll get it firsthand shortly."

Hurrying to her desk, she tossed her purse into the corner and sat down. *How could she not know what day it was or what she was supposed to be doing?* Her phone buzzed, signaling to her the work day was about to begin and her boss wanted her already. Hitting the intercom button, she let out a silent breath. "Morning, Wes."

"Teeg, I can't find the layouts for the sports blitz… did I give them to you?"

She flipped through the folders on her desk until she found them. "Got it right here."

"Good, it's due by the end of the day."

"No problem. I just have to get Ann to finish up a few font changes."

"Bring it when it's finished."

She nodded even though he couldn't see her. "Okay." Clicking the button off again, she leaned back and sighed. Her brain at least knew the right answers, even if she didn't. Grabbing the folder, she headed out into the art department. Of course, she could have called Ann from her desk, but she had to at least catch one glimpse of the new girl so her mind would leave that alone and let her get some work done.

Kat came around the corner and held out a cup. "I thought you could use a tea after your brisk start this morning."

Tucking the folder under her arm she accepted the cup and cradled it between her palms before inhaling the steam. "Thanks." Blowing on it, she started walking again. "Ann in work mode yet?"

Kat snorted. "More like wrath mode…"

"What? Why?"

Kat looked at the floor as someone walked by. "They put the new girl in her space."

"Oh. Bad."

"Yeah and then some."

"I'll see what I can do."

Kat grinned wide. "Thought you might Miss Director, can't have your top graphics designer on the warpath."

As they reached Ann's room, a tall redhead came strutting out. She brushed right past Teegan, almost causing her to wear her tea. With her mouth hanging open she turned to watch the woman in the too-tight red skirt wiggle her way down the corridor.

"That was the new girl, Celia Barnes," Kat whispered.

"You've got to be kidding me." Obviously, the material binding her butt in was under a lot of pressure, it looked like it didn't even move when she did.

"Nope."

"No wonder Ann is hissing."

"I am not hissing. I'm pissed. There is a difference." Ann leaned against the door and watched the redhead disappear around the corner.

"You wanted help…"

"Help doesn't mean I have to share my space, Teeg."

Teegan watched the way the redhead's hips swayed in the tight skirt, everything she disliked about some women was right there. *Hope she trips.* As if she'd pushed a button the woman stumbled over an invisible bump on the carpet. *Maybe today won't be so bad after all.* Smirking, she cleared her throat and turned back to Ann. "I'll talk to Wes and see if there is somewhere else we can put her."

Ann beamed at her. "Thanks." She pulled the folder out of her hand. "This the blitz layouts? I have some ideas..."

"Teegan."

Turning she spotted Wes standing at the door of his office. "Yes." Beside her Ann would be purring, she had a thing for the blond Greek god-like superior. Trying to see him from Ann's yummy classification scale didn't work for her. He was just Wes, her boss, confidant, and blond pretty boy. Dark and dangerous was what set her motor humming, unfortunately, there were no men in that group here at work... or anywhere that she'd ever found.

"Can you gather everyone to meet in the boardroom in an hour? I have an announcement." Adding his best pretty-boy smile, knowing that she didn't like unplanned meetings he turned and went back through the door.

Kat leaned closer. "What announcement?"

Gnawing on her lower lip for a few seconds, Teegan shook her head. "No idea, but I'm going to go find out."

Wes was sitting behind his desk looking at his watch as she came through the door. "That was fast, less than two minutes."

What was with everyone timing her today? Closing the door behind her, Teegan leaned back against it. "Announcement?"

"I'm great today, thanks for asking." He flashed a bright smile.

"Teeg, I can't find the layouts for the sports blitz..." Grimacing at her own imitation of him, she pushed away from the door and headed over to the chairs. "Sorry, it's been one of those days from the second my eyes opened."

Frowning, he leaned forward and studied her. "Everything all right?"

"Just another bad night, at least I think it was bad." *Did she tell him she had changed clothes in her sleep?*

He stood up and moved around to lean on the desk. "Dreams are back?"

"Yeah, and they're crazier than before."

The concern on his face was evident. "Have you been back to the doctor?" She shrugged. "Maybe you need to see a new doctor?"

Standing up, she went over and stood right in front of him. "Maybe you should stop procrastinating and trying to distract me and tell me what this announcement is all about."

He laughed. "Busted." His face went serious again. "Joking aside, don't let this get out of control. I am going to need you on top of your game for the next while."

"Why? What's going on?" She didn't try to hide the suspicion in her voice.

"One of the top board members is going to be working with us."

Groaning loudly, she dropped her head down almost to her chest. "Why?" She whined.

Wes laughed softly again and lifted her chin so she was looking at him again. "Because there are going to be some changes shortly and he's here to assess the situation." She feigned a pout as he held her face.

"Am I interrupting?"

They jumped apart and turned towards the man standing at the door. Wes cleared his throat. "No, come in."

Teegan's heart was in her throat as she studied the man entering the room. He moved like a predatory animal stalking his prey as he took long strides towards her boss. He had shoulder-length jet black hair that was combed back behind his head, so not the style she was used to seeing on men wearing two-thousand-dollar suits. Beneath the suit there were well-disciplined muscles, absent from any unnecessary handles, at least judging by the way he moved that was what he hid under the tailored cloth.

She stifled the urge to be as dramatic as Ann and wave a hand in front of her face. His jaw was broad and could have been molded from steel, from the angle she was getting. As she moved to his eyes, her heart skipped a few beats, dark and dangerous was the assessment her mind came up with. She also noticed those eyes were studying her as aptly as she was him. A man that masculine should be illegal. Sin in a suit was what this man was.

"Teegan." She turned to look at Wes when she realized he was speaking to her. "This is Leland McKay, the board member we were just discussing."

Swallowing, she debated for thirty seconds on whether she should speak or extend her hand. Both, she decided as she held out her hand to him. "Teegan Jacobs." As his large hand closed around hers, shocks buzzed up her arm. Pulling her hand away quickly she met his eyes to see the humor in them. *What was that?*

"The amazing director you were telling me about? I look forward to working with you."

When he smiled, she forgot any of the words she was about to speak.

Wes chuckled. "Be warned, Leland, stay out of her path when the deadlines are close, she'll run down anyone in her way."

Dragging her eyes away from the man, she glared at Wes. "Speaking of that, I have to go see if Ann has gotten anywhere with those changes." *Get away from him.* Giving the sexy giant a wide berth, she smiled sweetly. "Pleasure to meet you. I'll have everyone in the boardroom in forty-five minutes." He inclined his head but didn't speak.

As soon as the door closed, Leland turned back to Wes. "She's the one." It wasn't a question, for he'd felt her power as soon as he touched her.

"Yeah."

Leland smirked, "And do I want to know why you were holding her when I walked in?"

Wes snorted, "That wasn't holding her. She wasn't happy when I told her about you."

"Ah." Unbuttoning his jacket, he put his hands in his pockets. "Is there a connection between the both of you?"

Wes shook his head and leaned back against the desk. "Not the kind you think. We're friends, nothing more."

"Good." Moving over, he studied the picture on the wall. "The other one arrived this morning?"

Wes blew out a breath. "Yes, Celia is here now and the energy coming off her is darker than anything I've felt before."

"The council thought it would be strong." Turning he sent the other man a serious look. "And where is Teegan with everything? Has she realized yet?"

"No, but she's close. The dreams are coming to her..." Rubbing a hand over his jaw, he sighed. "I'm worried about her, she's fighting it every step of the way."

"That's why I'm here, it's my place to bring her to realize and accept her destiny."

Chortling, Wes walked back around behind his desk. "I wish you all the luck in the world, you're going to need it."

"I don't need luck, my friend, I have magic." Leland grinned wide. "I felt her magic with my own as soon as we touched."

Wes shook his head. "Years of training isn't going to help. You can't force anything on Teeg, she's a fighter, you're going to have to get her to trust you… and that, my friend, is a chore. I've been working with her for three years and it's just the past year she doesn't look at me like I'm a bug she'd like to squash."

Leland studied him for a long silent moment. "We'll see about that."

HEART

Animal Senses Book 1

JACQUELINE PAIGE

Chapter One

Blinking, Rayne glanced around. She was in the underground parking space in her apartment building and didn't even remember the drive. Her chest hurt, her hands were vibrating and reality felt far away. Three times, she tried to extract the keys from the ignition, and finally after fumbling she managed. *Come on, Rayne, get it together. Think!*

Her mind didn't want to accept the words that had come from Aiden's mouth, her fiancé. In all the years she'd known him, never had he used that tone. Scared her enough to send chills through her spine. She believed he meant every word. *I am not an idiot, I've always known he was a hard man, but the words turned my blood to ice and a part of me knows I'll never feel the same for him again.*

Taking a shaky breath, she groped around for her purse, feeling like she was moving through mud. Somehow, she managed to move and get out of the car. Her legs still felt like rubber, but she couldn't stay in the parking garage all day. Turning, she forced herself to move to the door.

What am I going to do? I can't marry a man like that. I'm not even sure if I can look at him now.

Stopping, she looked at the elevator door. Just the thought of stepping inside left her feeling suffocated and trapped. Hugging the purse again, she turned toward the stairwell. *Keep moving*—she had to.

Trapped, I am, aren't I? Trapped in a relationship. Just that one word showed her the next move. She had to get out of this relationship. Aiden was not her dream man if such a thing existed, but he had been comfortable. Admitting that, she now accepted that the relationship was too comfortable to be real.

When she reached her third-floor apartment, she wasn't out of breath. But, as numb as she felt, she wasn't sure if she *was* breathing. Maybe this was just a dream and she'd wake up any second now. Giving herself a small reprieve, she let that thought marinate for a few seconds before reality came crashing back.

It took her two tries to get the key into the lock. *What had his associate said just before my world darkened? "We haven't found a body or any sign of him, Aiden."* Him, who? A body? *A body!*

As Rayne stepped inside her apartment the dreamlike veil lifted away, revealing reality. *A reality I'm not sure how I can live with.* She quickly locked the door, all three locks. Not it would protect her, Aiden had keys. Leaning back against the door she tried to calm down and think.

Aiden was some sort of mob, mafia...*whatever?* Standing there she waited to feel her doubts were unsubstantiated, but it didn't happen. Her fear *was* the truth. This explained the dangerous-looking misfits he had in his employ. They had never quite *fit* she thought. Aiden wasn't a boy scout—she knew that. He was a powerful man, as his father had been, but what kind of power was now very clear to her. Closing her eyes, Rayne held a trembling hand over her heart, it was still beating too heavily. *I can't look at him again. Ever.* This only meant one thing...

She looked around the pretty apartment for a moment, taking two steps towards the kitchen before stopping. She had to leave, now. Everything was *his. He* paid for everything in this apartment, she worked in *his* gallery. Her whole world was controlled by *him*...

Moving in a slow circle, Rayne studied everything in sight. Every. Single. Thing.

Bought by him, in one way or another. Taking a deep breath, she tried to exhale slowly. Failing, her breath huffed out in one loud whoosh. There was no alternative, she had to get out of here.

Today.

Right now.

Kicking off her shoes, she bent down, scooped them up, and headed toward the bedroom.

Faster than she ever changed before, the skirt was stripped off and tossed on the bed. Barely having both legs in her jeans, Rayne began pulling open drawers and cabinets, dumping the contests all over the bed. All she really owned were clothes, her beloved camera, a laptop, and a few mementos to remind her of her parents. All of it was going in her car. A thought made her freeze as she held the empty drawer over the bed—her car was in *his* name. Dropping the drawer on the pile, Rayne sat on the bed, defeated. In the mirror, a frightened woman stared back. Seeing herself was enough to jolt her back into action. Giving the frail-looking reflection a determined nod, she made a solid decision. To hell with him. She was taking the car. He hated it, called it girlie, and complained it wasn't comfortable. *The car is now mine.*

Forty-five minutes later Rayne surveyed the bedroom. There was nothing left that she wanted. Leaning down and picking up the last bag, she went to set it with the rest. "This is pathetic, Rayne Andrews. Your entire life fits in six cases and a couple of purses."

She walked through the apartment for the last time, working out how to get all of the cases downstairs to the car without causing suspicion, when the ring of her cell phone pierced the silence. She looked over at her purse, the ringtone was Aiden's. A few seconds after it stopped, the phone on the table began to ring. *Can I do this?* Taking a deep breath, "Buy some time," she whispered aloud just before answering it.

"Hello?"

"There you are. You didn't answer your cell."

He may be using that soft tone, but she now *knew* what he was. "Oh, I was taking the garbage to the garbage room." Her hand shook as she held the phone and prayed that her voice didn't give anything away.

"Where the hell is that girl I pay to do that?"

Just the way he said it made her tremble. "I-it's Wednesday, Aiden. She doesn't come in today."

"Right. Listen baby, I may be here awhile. Could be most of the night..."

"That's—fine. I was heading to the spa shortly." Closing her eyes, she waited to see if he questioned that.

"Do you want me to come by in the morning to pick you up?"

For what? "Pick me up?"

He chuckled. "We have a brunch with Donny and his wife."

Letting out the silent breath she'd been holding. "Oh, yes please." *Please let me sound normal.*

"Okay baby. You go get all beautiful for me and I'll see you in the morning. Ten o'clock."

"Okay, Aiden."

"Love ya, baby."

"Me too." She hung up quickly. Suddenly gasping for air, Rayne tried to settle her nerves again. *Ten o'clock.* Looking over at the clock and doing the math, she had seventeen hours to disappear.

It took almost as long to get all the bags down as it had for her to pack them. Of course, if you're planning to pack your whole life up and vanishing, it would probably be easier if you didn't drive a *Cabriolet*. Fitting everything into the micro-sized car had taken more than one attempt. In the time it took to finish, she was much calmer about her decision to leave. Not that she had a choice, but she could always have a mini breakdown and cry her heart out, later. Right now, she needed a plan to figure out the next step.

The first stop was the gas station. Getting out of the car, she looked around, checking for Aiden or one of his men. *Great, paranoia already.* After she assured herself that he couldn't possibly know yet, Rayne walked over to the pump. As she lifted the card up to the slot, she realized that he could track her cards. As if the machine was going to grab it, she jerked her hand back and turned to get her purse. She'd need all the cash she had available. Looking over her shoulder again, she walked to the cash machine. This location was close enough to the apartment to not point in any direction—when she finally decided on which direction. Her hands weren't the steadiest as she punched in the numbers and requested the limit the machine would allow, the shaking increased when she grabbed the cash and stuffed it in her wallet.

Glancing around, she walked back to the pump, inserting a card to pay for the gas. It only took her a few minutes to decide she would hit a few more cash machines in the area to bypass withdrawal limits. Aiden might not drive by, but now she suspected he had people everywhere that would recognize her.

After the gas was pumped, she thought that a map would be a good thing, unless she planned to drive around Chicago endlessly—because that's the only place she'd ever driven. Reaching down, Rayne pulled out the nearest one, only to put it right back, it was a map of the one place she knew. Bending down, she studied the title of each map before spotting an oversized atlas with Canada in it. She grabbed that one. Before she could second guess the decision, she set it on the counter and waited for the clerk to ring it in.

With the receipt and atlas clutched in her vibrating hand, she went back to the car, hoping she could get through the next few moments without questioning what she was going to do next.

An hour later, she sat in an empty parking lot, trying to force a bagel down her throat. The atlas she'd purchased was propped against the steering wheel, endless lines of varying colors stared back at her. So many places and no idea where to go. She looked over at the glove box where she'd put her money—in a make-up bag no less. It had taken five different bank machines to empty her accounts of every cent she had. Her cards were now at their limits, accounts were empty and on a whim, Rayne had taken out a cash advance on the card Aiden had given her for emergencies. If this wasn't considered an emergency, she didn't know what was.

Focus, Rayne. Looking back at the map, she tried to wash down a bite with the lukewarm coffee. She knew making maps took a lot of work and was complicated in a way she didn't really care to understand, but they really weren't telling her anything. She needed her laptop and the internet to make a decision that the squiggly color co-ordinated lines weren't telling her. Sighing, she glanced around the parking lot. A hotel was at the far end. She reached down to pull the laptop case off the floor. Setting it on the passenger's seat, she opened it and hit the power button, praying for it to pick up a signal as she flipped through another few pages. There was a signal, not a strong one, but it would do. Bringing up a mapping site, she entered Chicago as the starting point. *Now what?* A starting point generally meant you needed a destination and that she didn't have. Flipping a few more pages, Rayne picked the first name that jumped off the page. Destination? Timmins, Ontario, Canada. Her heart was pounding as she hit enter.

Strangely, she felt relieved knowing she had decided on a location. Her resolve only faltered for a few seconds when she discovered there was a fourteen-hour drive to get there. Biting her lip, she looked out the windshield, not really focusing on anything. Was she ready for a fourteen-hour drive that would take her far away from Aiden? If she had translated the map correctly, where she was heading was right in the middle of nowhere. That meant there was less chance of her being found. Yes, she was ready. Picking up the notebook that was waiting for the details of *the* game plan, she started to jot down the directions, deciding after a few lines that she'd only write down the first five hours and then reassess her route from that point. She had no idea what it was going to be like driving this far.

Closing the laptop, she put it back on the floor and just sat there. Was she crazy for doing this? Yes, but she couldn't stay here and that left few options. She was alone, just like when her parents died. This time all the decisions to be made were going to be her own.

~

Her eyes felt completely dried out. Was such a thing even possible? She didn't know, but at the first drug store, she was getting some eye drops. Glancing at the time— again, Rayne squinted back at the road. *How long have I been driving now?* Four hours? No, closer to five, she needed to stop soon. A few hours ago, she had foolishly thought she would be across the border before planning a stop, but that wasn't going to happen. Driving at this speed meant she still had at least an hour and a half to go before reaching Mackinaw City and then another hour to the border. Considering the longest she'd ever driven passed an hour back, Rayne knew she wasn't going to make it. She had a newfound respect for people that drove for a living. The quick bathroom stop a few hours before hadn't been long enough. If she didn't stop soon, she was going to make mistakes and end up lost, or worse. Stopping would be for the best.

Blinking quickly, she tried to make her eyes not feel as dry and then focused on the sign she was coming to. A motel was thirty miles from here. Looking at the speedometer, Rayne attempted to do the math and calculate how long that would take, less than a minute later she gave up and decided it wasn't important. As long as she arrived at the motel before falling asleep. A few hours of rest, something to eat, and a shower became the new goal.

After what felt like ten hours she could see the hotel's sign not too far ahead. Elation and a bit of pride filled her as she realized she'd made it to here without help. She was slowing down when she noticed two police cars sitting at the motel. All the hair on the back of her neck stood up. Aiden couldn't know she was gone already, could he? Would he involve the police? Biting down on her lip, she thought he probably wouldn't, but she wasn't going to take any chances. Gripping the steering wheel tighter, her heart was crashing against her ribs at the thought that Aiden might find her. There would be more motels further away, and another chance to take a break.

It took several seconds for the sign she'd just passed to register. *I've done it!* She was almost to Mackinaw, at least that's what the sign had said. Taking a deep breath and fighting the grogginess that had been closing in for hours, she forced herself to keep going. Maybe a little air would help, not that it had a half hour ago, but it couldn't hurt. She rolled the window down, hoping it would help. Seven hours of driving, minus two very brief bathroom breaks and a stop for gas, and she'd managed to keep going. If she wasn't ready to pass out, she would be pretty impressed with what she'd managed.

After a few minutes of taking deep breaths she groaned, the open window wasn't working. Reaching for the radio, she fumbled with the buttons and flicked through the few stations that were clear, anything to sing to or even pretending to sing might work. She scowled at the radio. Turning it off, she stared at the road once again. "Okay," she tried to ignore how slurred her voice sounded. "Use your brain, get the blood pumping and drive." Wiggling a bit, she tried to sit straighter. "Great, my brain is already sleeping," she yawned while trying to see the sign that was getting closer. "Oh. Interstate one twenty-seven. I've been looking at that for what seems like forever," she mumbled to the eyes in the mirror. "And before that it was 131." She bobbed her head and tried to recall the roads before that. "One ninety...something, not that it matters really—It's not like I'm going to be going on the return trip," Rayne snorted and then laughed, not sure if it was delirium or exhaustion that had her talking to herself. "And what are you going to do when you reach your middle of nowhere in Canada, Ms. Andrews?" She glanced at the speedometer, even though she had no idea what it had said on the Mackinaw sign she'd just driven past. Clearing her throat, she looked at the reflection again. "I have no idea what I'm going to do. I didn't sit down and plot out a course of action before fleeing," she giggled quietly this time and then squealed as she drove by another sign. "What—ah, miles..." biting her lip a couple of times, she looked at the time. "Oh! A half hour!" Gripping the steering wheel with the very last of her energy, she focused on the road. "You did it. And the reward?" She attempted to smile but yawned and erased what would have been the smile. "The reward is sleep."

Rayne stood, clutching the room key in her hand and looking at the car, deciding. With the way she'd stuffed the cases into the car, there was no easy way to get to the one that had the clothes she wanted, without taking everything out of the car. Did she care if she slept in something fresh? At this point, no, she would come back out later and sort out what to change into. As she started to head for the room, her brain flashed a warning. She wasn't feeling very trusting now. Turning back, she unlocked the car and reached in to grab her purse, money, camera, and laptop. If anyone decided to pick up the tiny car and carry it away, she could get by with just this.

Stumbling into the dark room, she kicked the door closed. Her shoes were off in two steps, it felt glorious. Her leg smacked into the bed. Setting the precious items down on it, she shoved them to the other side and flopped down, face first. Had she asked for a wake-up call? The chances of a yes were high, but there was no way she could summon the energy to find out.

The Huntress

Alterealm Series

Book 1

By J. Risk

Chapter One

I didn't even get both eyes opened and focused before I knew something was wrong. Where was the color? I was only seeing sepia? Everything was brown. Blinking rapidly, I tried to readjust my eyes to see if there was any other hue. It didn't change a thing and for the life of me I couldn't figure out why.

Sitting there, I tried to decipher what was going on and why I was sitting on the ground. Looking down I ran my hand over the dried dusty surface. Why was I on the ground? Craning my neck as far as I could in all directions, I looked around. Okay, where was the pavement and cement? The buildings and streets I called my natural turf?

The why's flying around in my brain suddenly decided the top question, was what the *hell* was going on?

Squeezing my eyes shut, I struggled to recall the last thing I remembered doing. I was hunting down a bounty—a nice one with a large dollar sign attached to her. I had tracked her ass down and...

Did I confront her? Yes, I was minutes away from calling Frank and telling him to get out his shiny pen and sign my check.

So what happened between then and now? Not to sound repetitive, which is something that drives me nuts, but *what* the hell was going on?

Startled, I started to check for bullet holes or the deep crevices that knives leave behind in flesh. That had to be it, I'd taken a beating and this was that in-between place you sit when you're near death's door, but not quite ready to see what lies on the other side.

Finding no critical injury, I slumped forward and rubbed my head. There was some rational explanation for this, there had to be. Had I been drugged? It could be some crazy hallucination. Any minute now I was going to either wake up in my bed at home or some hospital with a cheery nurse leaning over me, reassuring me we are going to be *just* fine. I only had to wait it out a little longer and all would be normal.

To kill time until I woke up, I looked around some more. Wherever this was it looked like a burnt-out world. Not the charred kind of burn, but depleted and completely used up sort.

Vacant.

Sitting still wasn't really a strong trait of mine, so I figured I'd get up and take a look around, there had to be something to see around here. If my body was actually somewhere else for safekeeping, what harm could come to me, right?

I staggered like I'd never stood before, struggling to get my balance. Whatever was going on with me, my equilibrium was totally shot. Standing there swaying like grass in the breeze, I turned carefully trying to see if there was anything around me except rust-tinted dirt and nothingness.

My heart stumbled around in my chest when I spotted someone coming in my direction. Yes! I wasn't the only one in this soulless place.

The closer it got to me made me the more I questioned my original conclusion. I didn't know, exactly, but it was not some*one* it was a some*thing*. No one label could describe it. Standing over six feet, it had the shape of a man dressed in jeans and a large, very out-of-fashion gingham snap up shirt. When I reached the face, I can only describe it as part wrinkled puppy dog with floppy skin crossed with Freddy and Jason after the slash scenes.

It stopped in front of me and instinct had me reach around behind me under my jean jacket for my raptor claw knife, which I put on as regular as underwear when dressing; and that would be every day, by the way. Relief washed over me when I felt the small circular handle. At least while waiting to survive I got to bring my toys with me.

Big brown eyes assessed me slowly and I wanted to make the call that it was harmless, but yeah, having tracked down anything from a sicko killer to a card shark in the last three years, I knew better than to fall for sappy looks.

"Are you a magishian? You juisht appeared."

A male voice, even though he spoke with a heavy lisp that randomly inserted *ish* into his words. Then again if I had saggy lips like he did, I'd be happy to talk at all. I sized him up for a few more seconds, trying to gauge whether he was really in front of me, or if I was having some sort of psychotic episode. Was a magician good or bad? I decided the play dumb, being blonde did have *some* advantages. "A magician?"

Those brown eyes developed a nervous quiver. Magician equaled bad. "No…"

He looked relieved. "Oh good. I didn't want to have to bash you over the head."

I grasped my raptor tightly and shrugged. "Yeah, me either."

The sky brightened and began to glow a rust orange color. When I asked for some color, I'd hoped for something out of the orange family.

"We better go, they'll be coming soon."

"They?" I glanced around quickly, not wanting to take my eyes off him for long.

He nodded and pranced on the spot, the nervous movement had me on high alert. "The daywalkers." He whispered.

Daywalkers? Did I even want to know? I didn't think so, but this bizarre nightmare wasn't going to be complete if I didn't ask.

Looking me over a few times, his eyes widened under the pressure of his drooping forehead; *that* was quite the expression. "You're not one of them, are you?"

I walked in the day, night and even at dusk, but I wasn't going to tell him that. I decided honesty might work, if not violence was always a good backup. Judging by his expression daywalker ranked on the bad list with magician. "I—I don't know what you'd call me."

Those sappy eyes looked me up and down a few times trying to figure me out. "You better come with me. It's not safe to leave you wandering around." He looked behind him and then motioned behind me and started walking.

I knew in my gut it was a mistake, but as I had no other real options… I didn't know where I was or what was going on and so far he knew more than I did. "Where are we going?"

Pausing he glanced over his shoulder and then lumbered along again. "I'll take you to Troy, he'll know what to do."

My eyes were starting to strain as the sky brightened. "This Troy, he's in charge?"

He stopped so suddenly I almost plowed right into his back. When he turned and looked at me, his eyes weren't a sad brown anymore but were leaning more towards red. It had to be from the strange color of the sunrise. "You're not from Alterealm are you?"

"Is that where we are?"

He nodded.

"Nope."

That nervous jitter of his seemed to return all at once. "How did you get here?"

A reasonable question that I had nothing to offer that resembled an answer. "I don't know that either."

His red eyes darted to the sky. "We have to go."

Turning, he began jogging toward, well, nothing that I could see. Not wanting to find out what he was afraid of, I ran along behind him. All I could think was this Troy person, if he was a person, better have some answers.

He stopped again and dropped down onto his knees. Was he hurt? Surely that short jaunt hadn't winded him that much. He began tapping his hand on the ground. What was he doing? Looking all around us, I kept watch for anything really, not wanting to meet these daywalkers in the slightest. Just when I'd had about enough of his short break, he grasped something in the sand and pulled a door in the ground open.

"We're going to have to use the shortcut. We don't have time to get to the main gates."

Looking down into a hole with a ladder, I glanced around again and despite every muscle in my body telling me to run and get the hell out of here, I started down the metal rungs into a deep hole that would take me, hopefully back to friggin' reality.

About Jacqueline Paige

I am a multi-published author of 'all things paranormal'. My book list proves this is my niche with my stories of witches, ghosts, psychics, shifters, and more now on the shelves. My current genres are paranormal romance, paranormal fantasy, and paranormal romantic suspense.
My books are available in many formats around the globe, including book/reading apps. Since adding them during the pandemic, my books have had over a million reads and my 'to be written' list is growing longer each day. I can't write fast enough.

I began my writing career in 2006 (as a joke) and my first book was published in 2009. I haven't stopped since then. I am an avid reader and will read 'anything with words', whether it's a novel, article, or even every sign I pass.

I live in Ontario, Canada in a small town that's part of the popular Georgian Triangle area. Even though I can see the mountains, I do not ski.

When I'm not in one of my writing worlds, I spend time with my grand-monsters. I have nine of them (so far) and I look forward to corrupting them in the years to come.
Jacqueline also writes under the pseudonym of J. Risk

Jacqueline loves to hear from her readers, you can find her at

http://jacquelinepaige.com/

Author note:

Did you enjoy reading one of my books?

If so, PLEASE help spread the word on social media. You can help by sharing on Facebook, tweet about it, post something on Instagram, Pinterest. Posting a review on your favorite book sites go a long way to help authors. With your help in keeping my books "out there", I can continue writing to keep those stories coming.

Writing and promoting can be very time consuming. I love talking to readers, but the hours spent on keeping so many social media outlets current can become overwhelming and time for writing pays the price. If you can take a few minutes to help, that would be awesome. Thank you!